Praise for **THE GOOD THIEVES**

'An amazing adventure story, told with sparkling style and sleight of hand'

Jacqueline Wilson

'A new Katherine Rundell book is always an event, but this is another triumph and then some. A wickedly exciting heist with heart, I can but marvel at this new delight from one of my favourite storytellers ever'

Kiran Millwood Hargrave

'A total showstopper of a story. Rundell's finest yet'

Emma Carroll

'I love the way Katherine puts Impossible on hold while she tells her wild, warm, shimmering stories'

Hilary McKay

'*The Good Thieves* is a storytelling spectacle – it glitters with adventure, family, friendship, and an irresistible sprinkling of impossibility'

Catherine Doyle

'I know the world will love it. It's full of mischief, vibrancy, tenacity and wonder'

Cerrie Burnell

The Good Thieves lights a spark in your heart from the very first line and sets it blazing with danger, daring, high-wire thrills and a vivid, unstoppable spirit of love and hope. I adored it'

Lauren St John

'Increasingly I feel that doctors should prescribe Katherine Rundell books to patients – all that wisdom, all that humour, all that irrepressible joy. *The Good Thieves* is, predictably, superb'

Abi Elphinstone

'A truly excellent book. Stolen castles, daring heists, prohibition, pickpockets, animal adventure, the circus, a truly terrifying villain, and four of the best protagonists I've ever encountered. Plus Katherine Rundell's glorious prose'

Katherine Webber

THE GOOD THIEVES

THE GOOD THIEVES

KATHERINE RUNDELL

ILLUSTRATED
BY
MATT SAUNDERS

BLOOMSBURY
CHILDREN'S BOOKS
LONDON   OXFORD   NEW YORK   NEW DELHI   SYDNEY

BLOOMSBURY CHILDREN'S BOOKS
Bloomsbury Publishing Plc
50 Bedford Square, London WC1B 3DP, UK
29 Earlsfort Terrace, Dublin 2, Ireland

BLOOMSBURY, BLOOMSBURY CHILDREN'S BOOKS and the Diana logo
are trademarks of Bloomsbury Publishing Plc

First published in Great Britain in 2019 by Bloomsbury Publishing Plc
This edition published in Great Britain in 2020 by Bloomsbury Publishing Plc

A catalogue record for this book is available from the British Library

ISBN: HB: 978-1-4088-5489-1; PB: 978-1-4088-8265-8;
eBook: 978-1-4088-5490-7

6 8 10 9 7 5

Typeset by RefineCatch Limited, Bungay, Suffolk
Printed and bound in Great Britain by CPI Group (UK) Ltd, Croydon CR0 4YY

To find out more about our authors and books visit www.bloomsbury.com
and sign up for our newsletters

To Ellen Holgate, my editor,
and Claire Wilson, my agent.
What luck, to work with two such women

CHAPTER ONE

Vita set her jaw and nodded at the city in greeting, as a boxer greets an opponent before a fight.

She stood alone on the deck of the ship. The sea was wild and stormy, casting salt spray thirty feet into the air, and all the other passengers on the ocean liner, including her mother, had taken sensible refuge in their cabins.

But it is not always sensible to be sensible.

Vita had slipped away and stood out in the open, gripping the rail with both hands as the boat crested

1

a wave the size of an opera house. So it was that she alone had the first sight of the city.

'There she is!' called a deck hand. 'In the distance, port side!'

New York climbed out of the mist, tall and grey-blue and beautiful; so beautiful that it pulled Vita forwards to the bow of the boat to stare. She was leaning over the railing, as far out as she dared, when something came flying at her head.

She gasped and ducked low. A seagull was chasing a young crow across the sky, pecking at its back, wheeling and shrieking in mid-air. Vita frowned. It wasn't, she thought, a fair fight. She felt in her pocket, and her fingers closed on an emerald-green marble. She took aim, a brief and angry calculation of distance and angle, drew back her arm, and threw.

The marble caught the seagull on the exact centre of the back of its skull. The gull gave the scandalised cry of an angry duchess, and the crow spun in the air and sped back towards the skyscrapers of New York.

*

They took a cab from the docks. Vita's mother carefully counted out a handful of coins, and gave the driver the address. 'As close as we can get for that, please,' she said, and he took in her carefully mended hems and nodded.

Manhattan sped past outside the window, bright bursts of colour amid the storm-beaten brick and stone. They passed a cinema, its walls adorned with pictures of Greta Garbo, and a man selling hot lobster claws out of a cart. A tram thundered past at a crossroads, narrowly missing a van advertising *The Colonial Pickle Works*. Vita breathed in the city. She tried to memorise the layout of the streets, to build a map behind her eyes; she whispered the names: *'Washington Street, Greenwich Avenue.'*

When the money ran out, they walked. They went as fast as Vita could go in the ferocious wind, suitcases in hand, along Seventh Avenue, dodging pinstripe men and sharp-heeled women.

'There!' said Vita's mother. 'That's Grandpa's flat.'

The apartment building on the corner of Seventh and West 57th rose up, tall and stately in brown stone, from the busy pavement. A newspaper boy stood outside, roaring the headlines into the wind.

Across the road from the apartment block was a light-red-brick building, its facade arched and ornamented. Flagpoles protruded from its wall, and two flags flapped wildly. Above them, picked out in coloured glass, were the words 'Carnegie Hall'.

'It all looks very ... smart,' said Vita. The apartment block appeared to purse its lips at the world. 'Are you *sure* this is the place?'

'I'm sure,' said her mother. 'He's on the top floor, right under the roof. It used to be the maid's apartment. It'll be a squeeze, but it's not for long.' Their return ticket was booked for three weeks' time. Enough time, said Vita's mother, to sort out Grandpa's papers, pack his few things, and persuade him to come home with them.

'Come on!' Her mother's voice sounded unnaturally bright. 'Let's go and find him.'

The lift was broken, so Vita half ran up the stairs to Grandpa's apartment, jerkily, as fast as her legs would take her. Her suitcase banged against the walls as she raced up narrow flights of stairs, ignoring the growing pain in her left foot. She came to rest, breathless, outside the door. She knocked, but there was no response.

Vita's mother came, panting, up the final flight of stairs. She bent to pick the apartment key from under the mat. She hesitated, looking down at her daughter. 'I'm sure he won't be as bad as we feared,' she said, 'but—'

'Mama! He's waiting!'

Her mother opened the door, and Vita went tearing down the hall; and then, in the doorway, she froze.

Grandpa had always been thin; handsome and lean, with long fine hands and shrewd blue-green eyes. Now he was gaunt, and his eyes had drawn back into his skull. His fingers had drawn inwards into fists, as if every part of him was pulling back from the world. A walking stick leaned against the wall next to his chair: he hadn't needed a walking stick before.

He had not seen her and, just for that second, his face looked sculpted from solid grief.

'Grandpa!' said Vita.

But then he turned, and his face was transfigured with light, and she could breathe again.

'Rapscallion!' He stood and Vita hurled herself into his arms, and he laughed, winded by the impact.

'Julia,' he said, as Vita's mother came in, 'I only got your telegram three days ago, or I would have stopped you—'

Vita's mother shook her head. 'Just try to hold us back, Dad.'

Grandpa turned to Vita. 'Smile again for me, Rapscallion?'

So she smiled, at first naturally, and then, when he didn't look away, wider, until it felt like every single one of her teeth was showing.

'Thank you, Rapscallion,' he said. 'You have your grandmother's smile, still.' Vita's stomach clenched as she saw tears rise up in her grandfather's eyes.

'Grandpa?'

He coughed, and smiled, and cleared his throat. 'God, it's good to see you. But there was no need.'

Julia pushed Vita towards the door. 'Go and find your room, darling,' she said.

'But—'

'Please,' said her mother. Her face was white, and exhausted. 'Now.'

'It's the one at the end of the corridor,' said Grandpa. 'More of a cupboard than a room, I'm afraid,' he said, 'but the view is very fine.'

Vita went slowly down the corridor, her suitcase in hand. She noticed how the floorboards squeaked; how the paint peeled from the wall. She pushed at the door. It stuck; she held on to the wall and kicked it with her stronger foot. It flew open, scattering thin shards of plaster.

The room was so small she could practically touch all four walls at once, but it had a wooden wardrobe, and a window looking out over the street. Vita sat on the bed, pulled off her left shoe, and took her foot in both hands. She dug her fingers into the sole, pointing and flexing the toes, and tried to think.

They had arrived. She should be thrilled. They had made it across the ocean, halfway around the world, and New York waited outside the window, stretching up to the sky like the calligraphy of a particularly flamboyant god.

But none of that mattered at all, because Grandpa wasn't as bad as she had feared. He was worse.

Vita's skirt pockets were full of gravel from the garden back home; she picked out the largest stones, and began to throw them at the wardrobe door. It helped her think.

A person watching might have noted that each hit the precise mathematical centre of the wardrobe handle – but nobody was watching, and Vita herself barely noticed. Her mind was not on the stones.

She had to do something to make it right. She did not yet know what, nor how, but love has a way of leaving people no choice.

CHAPTER TWO

Grandpa's disaster had come from a blue sky, as disaster often does. The telegram he sent Vita's mother had been short: YOUR MUM DIED LAST NIGHT.

Vita had sat on the doormat, unable to move. Her mother, white-faced, carried her into bed, where together they drank blackcurrant cordial and told each other stories of Grandma, who had travelled the world with Grandpa and had a guttural laugh like a sailor's. The stories helped them both a little, as stories often do.

But that had not been the end of it. More letters followed. The first were dark, and short. Hudson Castle, Grandpa wrote, felt full of ghosts.

Hudson Castle was very small, judging by castle standards. It had been uprooted from its hilltop in France and shipped, stone by stone, across the ocean to America by Vita's great-great-great-grandfather. The castle had been thought, in its day, both very grand and mildly insane. Now it was run-down, crumbling, beautiful, and inhabited only by Grandpa, entirely alone.

But then hope had crept in. A man, Grandpa wrote, had offered to rent Hudson Castle. He had offered to transform it into a school. Grandpa would stay on as a governor; it would give him new purpose, something to do. No paperwork had been signed, but the man was eager to begin renovations. The man's name was Sorrotore, a New York millionaire.

He enclosed a press cutting, showing a man standing outside a vast New York building, smiling at the camera with Hollywood teeth. 'Victor Sorrotore outside his home in the Dakota,' read the caption.

10

'Victor Sorrotore,' whispered Vita, and she memorised his face, just in case.

Within a week, Sorrotore struck. Grandpa returned from an afternoon walk to find his way back home barred. A strange man with two guard dogs came out of the caretaker's cottage and pointed a rifle at him. 'Hudson Castle belongs to Mr Sorrotore,' the guard had said. 'Scram!'

Grandpa had never in his adult life been told to scram. He had tried to push past the guard, and one of the dogs had bitten his ankle; not a snap but a true bite, which drew blood. The gun was levelled at his chest. Bewildered, he took the train to New York, rented the tiny apartment on Seventh Avenue, and found Sorrotore's lawyer.

The lawyer expressed surprise as only lawyers can, his eyebrows riding so high up his face they nearly reached the back of his neck. Grandpa knew very well, the lawyer said, that he had sold the castle to Sorrotore. The money was there, in Grandpa's account. A very small sum – only $200 – but it was understood that Hudson Castle had become a burden, one Grandpa was glad to be rid of. Grandpa checked his account; it was true.

Grandpa tried to hire a lawyer of his own, to demand that Sorrotore produce the title deeds, but he could find none who would take the case without more money than he had. 'Justice,' he wrote in his final letter, 'seems to be only for those who can afford it.' He would try, now, to forget the house in which he had been born. He would try, he wrote, to forget his life there with Lizzy: it was safer that way.

Upon receipt of this last letter, Vita's heart had swooped into her throat. Hudson Castle was Grandpa's home. It was where he could live alongside all his memories of Grandma Lizzy. 'No,' she whispered.

She had seen her mother's face, and it had given her hope. Her mother was soft-bodied, sweet-voiced, and iron-willed. The two shared the same brown eyes, and the same stubborn jawline.

The next day, her mother returned from town with two tickets in hand. 'We're bringing him back here, whether he likes it or not. The ship sails from Liverpool,' she had said. 'We leave tonight.'

Vita saw that her mother's engagement and wedding rings had gone from her left hand. She didn't ask more, only went to her bedroom to pack, her boots smacking on the floor like a soldier's on the way to battle.

It was Grandpa who taught Vita to throw.

Vita's grandfather's name was Jack Welles. Or, technically – because he had come from the kind of family that believed in long names, long cars, and long dinners – his name was William Jonathan Theodore Maximilian Welles. The family fortune had long since disappeared, but the habit of extravagant naming remained. His father was American, his mother and his schooling were English. Jack was a jeweller by trade, tall enough for doorways to pose a hazard, and thin enough to fit his legs through a letterbox.

When Vita was five, two things happened: her father was killed in the Great War, and she contracted polio. Her mother fought against the disease with wild, unsleeping passion. For long dark months Vita lay in a hospital bed, lifted out for baths in almond meal and oxidised water. She was given chloride of gold to drink, and wine of pepsin. She began to look far older than she was.

And then one day her grandparents arrived from America. Grandpa sat by her bed, gave her a ping-pong ball, and told her to call him when she could hit the head surgeon with it. Then he drew, with the steady hand of a jeweller, a very small bullseye on the far hospital wall.

She missed, and missed, until she did not.

Grandpa coached her like an athlete. He was a crack shot himself, and Vita spent hours throwing. She threw pebbles, marbles, darts, paper aeroplanes. When she came home from hospital, aged seven, she could send steak knives in elegant loops to land upright in a pat of butter across the room.

Vita grew, and her bones grew stronger, and eventually her leg brace was put away. Her left calf was thinner than her right, and her left foot curved in on itself, and her shoes were made, gratis, by a cobbler in the softest leather he could find. Her mother top-stitched them with red silk, and embroidered birds

14

on them. She could run, though it made the muscles pull and burn, and although Vita willingly complained of cuts, and demanded bandages where there was very little blood, she never breathed a word about that particular pain.

She grew up small, and still, and watchful. She had six kinds of smile, and five of them were real. All of them were worth seeing. Her hair was the reddish-brown of a freshly washed fox.

Vita's mother Julia only once raised the question of Vita's constant target practice.

'She won't have it easy,' said Grandpa. 'And she looks so breakable. She might as well know how to throw a rock or two.'

By the time Vita was eight, she could hit an apple in the highest branches of a tree from fifty paces. She could skim a stone and make it bounce twenty-three times. 'Back home, your Grandpa's the best shot in town,' said Grandma Lizzy. She was a tall woman, with a stern nose and richly kind eyes. 'But I think you're better.'

Grandpa watched Vita bowl overarm at the sea.

'Now learn about velocity: learn how the air makes things twist. Look it up! Learn it! Learn as much as you can, for learning is the very opposite of death! Wonderful!' Grandpa was the only person Vita knew who seemed to spark electricity when he talked, as if he struck against the world like flint against steel.

Eventually, Grandpa and Grandma went back to America, back to Hudson Castle. It was shortly after this that everything changed, and led Vita here, to her tiny room in the attic, looking out as the sun set over New York City.

CHAPTER THREE

The sky was moonless and starless that first night, but New York is never dark. Vita rose after midnight to find the city still awake. She crossed to the window; the apartment block was tall, taller than any around it, and she could see the streets below her stretching away towards the great darkness of Central Park. Street lamps, house lights, the basement-window blaze of illicit speakeasies, car headlamps, flashes of cigar-tips; Manhattan shivered and glowed.

Sleep, Vita felt, was impossible. There was a

restaurant in the building next door, and from it came the music of two violins, and loud, off-key male singing.

Across the street, the red brick of Carnegie Hall had turned to bronze under the street lights, its facade full of hushed solemnity. Then she blinked, and looked closer.

Right at that moment it was neither hushed nor solemn, because a boy was on the brink of jumping out of the third-floor window.

He clambered up and stood on the sill. He was thin, with dark skin and protruding ears, and he did not look down, but out, across the city.

A second, smaller boy came running round the edge of the building, laughing, dragging a thin mattress along the pavement in both hands. He dropped the mattress and called out.

'*Listo!* Ready! *Hep!*'

The boy on the window sill lifted his arms above his head and, before Vita could call out to him to stop, he threw himself upwards and outwards. Vita couldn't breathe. But he tucked his knees tight into his chest and spun twice in the air, unfurling himself rod-straight just in time to land, feet first, on the mattress. He took a step, toppled to his knees, and sprang up again. The smaller boy gave a shout of triumph, and the taller smiled a small half-smile.

Then he looked up and saw her leaning perilously far out of her window, the ledge cutting against her belly button. For one second all three faced each other, eyes wide in the night air. Then the taller boy smiled that same secret, private smile, and the smaller boy, seeing it, laughed and saluted. Just as Vita was going to shout down to them, both boys took off around the corner, the smaller boy dragging the mattress behind them.

Vita looked down at the pavement, but there was nobody in sight to confirm that a boy had, in fact, just taken flight.

'Remember them,' she whispered to herself. 'Just in case. Just in case.' As if she could have forgotten.

Vita woke on her first morning in New York to the sound of music outside her window. She spat on her finger to wipe the sleep out of her eyes, and peered out. A man in a hat pulled low over his eyes stood leaning against the tree on the pavement, working away at his barrel organ.

The day was sunlit and bright blue, but cold enough that her breath puffed out in clouds of mist as she washed and dressed in a warm knitted jersey and a bright red skirt she could kick in. She carefully buttoned on her red silk boots, and brushed her hair with her fingers.

In the drawing room Grandpa sat in the armchair, watching the sky. He turned round when she came in, and she saw the effort it took for him to arrange his features into his old smile.

'Rapscallion! Good morning. Your mother's left already, to go and speak to my bank manager, and see what can be done. She was wearing her most crusading expression.'

Vita nodded. Her mother, when she focused on something, pursued it with the unswerving determination of a warship.

'She said she's afraid she'll be out a lot, renewing

my passport, and transferring what's left of my bank account to a British one – and so I'm responsible for you and your movements. She made me promise that we would both be sensible.' He raised one quizzical eyebrow. 'Have you any plans for what your movements may be?'

Vita said, 'I'm going to make sausages with ketchup.' Ketchup was a revelation which she had discovered on the boat and eaten every day since. 'Would you like some?'

He shook his head. 'That's very kind, but not for me.'

'Or coffee?' Coffee, Vita knew, was what you were supposed to drink in America. It tasted, to her, like angry mud, but she was aware that others felt differently. 'I don't actually know how to make it, but I could try.'

'No, thank you.'

'There's nothing I can do?'

'Just you being here is enough.'

But it wasn't enough, she knew, because as she turned to the kitchen, she saw him lean back in his chair, and the hollow look come into his eyes.

She found sausages, and put them in the oven, and was just digging a knife into the ketchup bottle when she heard Grandpa call.

'Rapscallion? Are you still there?'

Vita went to his side, as fast as she could go. 'Yes!'

'Come and sit, while your sausages cook. There's something important I need to tell you.' Grandpa's eyes were staring past her, past the rooftops outside and past the city beyond, and they were angry.

'What is it?' When he did not answer, she sat down on the floor and laid one hand on his ankle. To have your ankle held, she had found, can help, if it is the right person doing the holding.

'I need you to listen,' he said. 'You always were a remarkable listener, Rapscallion. For your own safety, I need you to know about Sorrotore. And I need you to know about what he took.'

'Your grandma made the old castle come alive,' said Grandpa. 'She could grow things where no things should be able to grow. There were wild strawberries in the mouths of the gargoyles, roses up the burglar bars and in through the windows. There was an almost inconvenient amount of ivy growing up the toilet bowl.' He screwed his eyes shut, as if he could see it, and it hurt him.

'My great-grandfather would be ashamed of me,' said Grandpa. 'He thought, when he died, he left us in luxury – carriages, horses, jewels. The jewels! Diamonds, rubies, sapphires. It was almost all lost. My grandfather gambled away most of it. But what I've done is worse. I've lost our home. And, my God – what would Lizzy say, if she knew?'

'She would say it wasn't your fault,' said Vita sternly. 'I know it.'

'We had so much glory in us when we were young. The last jewel was a necklace – an emerald pendant, large as a lion's eye. We had it valued, when we needed money to mend the roof; it was worth thousands. Oh, Rapscallion – if you could have seen us! She'd put on her emerald, and we'd go out dancing.'

Vita tried to keep her face mute, unexcited. 'Did you say, thousands of dollars?'

'She looked so beautiful. I took a photograph of her in it – my Liz, she loved it …' He ceased speaking, and choked. 'When she died, I didn't know what to do – so I hid it. I couldn't bear to see it. It's still there, in the old hiding place. Oh, Vita.' He took a deep, shuddering breath, and tried to compose his face.

An emerald necklace. The thought ran like an electric shock through Vita's body. She could not take back a house; but an emerald was different. An emerald, as large as a lion's eye, worth thousands of dollars, could change everything.

I can get it back. I can steal it back.

And I could sell it. I could use the money for a lawyer and force them to give Grandpa back his home.

'It's impossible,' she told herself. *But*, whispered a small voice inside her, *impossible doesn't mean it's not worth trying*.

Vita placed an apple on top of the chest of drawers. She sat on her bed facing it, held her penknife in her hand, and focused on the very tip of the apple's stalk.

Colours flickered behind her eyes, and she pushed away her daily thoughts, the busy smallnesses, searching for the still steady place in her mind. Grandpa had always said, 'If you put your mind in a position where an idea can find you, an idea will always come eventually.'

'Of course,' he had added, 'the idea will not necessarily be practical, nor legal.'

The plan which began to take shape in her mind was neither.

She sat for a long time, staring straight ahead, barely breathing. She had never been so still in her life. The constant, thrumming pain in her foot no longer reached her. She thought her way around corners and back out of dead ends.

The plan took on capital letters and italics in her head. It became solid.

Vita blinked, and shook herself. She flicked open the blade of her penknife, and threw it hard across the room; the handle was weighted unevenly and it spun, yet the blade sank with a thud in the very heart of the apple. The apple toppled on to the floor.

Vita smiled one of her six smiles. Then she took from her luggage a red notebook, and, her eyes still hot with concentration, she wrote two words:

THE PLAN.

She underlined them.

Next she flipped the book upside down, to begin on a blank page from the other side, and started to write:

The day Grandpa and Grandma went back to America was the day I got my penknife.

I didn't want to watch them go, so I went to the woods to be alone. I was trying to hit a knot in a tree with a handful of stones, but I kept missing; I couldn't see.

A voice behind me said, 'Concentrate.'

And I said, 'I am!'

He said, 'You're sad, Rapscallion, and angry. I know. But if you can learn to transform anger and sadness into something – into work, into kindness – then you will be remarkable. Put your sadness and anger into your wrist, and throw it.'

'How?' I said. 'I don't see how.'

He said, 'It's a trick that takes a lifetime to learn. Try again. Imagine shifting your sadness out of your chest and into your hand. Throw.'

I tried. I pushed my heart down into my hand, and threw the stone, and I hit the knot, right in the middle of the tree. I turned round, and there he was, sitting on a tree stump and smiling. And he said, 'Close your eyes.'

And he put a red penknife into my hand.

He said, 'It was mine, when I was your age. It's called a Swiss Army knife. To remind you, you are an army unto yourself.'

I opened it. It was perfectly oiled. A long blade, scissors, a pair of detachable tweezers tucked into the top.

'Use it as a tool, not a weapon,' he said. 'Your weapon in life is not going to be a knife – it will be something far more powerful and original. But the tweezers will come in handy. Good tweezers are not to be underestimated.'

And he kissed the top of my head and walked away without saying anything.

That's the kind of man that Grandpa was, before Grandma died. Before Sorrotore.

Vita drew a line under her writing, and put the book away under her pillow.

She did not remember the sausages until much later, and although by then they were largely charcoal, she ate them anyway, with plenty of ketchup, followed by the apple. The plan had brought back her appetite, as plans so often do.

CHAPTER FOUR

Later that day, Vita crept out of the apartment, leaving Grandpa sleeping, and took a cab. She took it alone, which she had never done before, and she took it with her fists balled up inside her coat pockets and her heart beating hard.

Her first attempt to summon a cab had failed; she stood on the street outside Carnegie Hall, holding up her thumb, but when the driver who slowed saw there was no adult with her, he swerved away and drove on. On her second attempt, she wrenched open the door and threw herself into the back seat before the driver could leave without her.

She pressed her face against the glass. It was early evening and the streets were crowded. The car hurtled across 59th Street and up Central Park West, the lights of a cinema illuminating the name of a film, *Wild Bill Hickok*.

Vita felt the bite and kick of New York spark through her. She reached into her pocket. There was a map of the city, borrowed from her grandfather, and, under it, her penknife. She closed her fingers around it, and it gave her courage.

Abruptly the cab pulled up beside the pavement. 'This is you, kid,' said the driver. 'The Dakota!'

He told her the cost for the journey, which sounded enormous. Vita knew Americans tipped everyone, but had no idea how much, so it seemed safest to give him all the money she had with her and dart away down the pavement.

She stood looking up at the building. It was vast; a castle of a place, with crenellations and turrets in the four corners, and light pouring from its windows.

As she stood there, a grey-haired man and a tall woman swept past her. The wind rose in a sudden gust and the woman laughed, lifting her hand to her hair, which was swept up with a diamond-studded swan's feather.

'Do try not to be dull, honey, or talk endlessly about politics,' said the woman. She spoke with a strong New York accent. 'Victor's parties are always so fabulously *it*.'

Vita's heart swooped with the luck of it. She didn't let herself hesitate – she followed them, keeping as close as she dared. The man and woman passed through a door, nodded at a doorman (Vita nodded too, trying to make her smile doorman-appropriate) and got into a lift. Vita stepped in with them, attempting to look haughty and unconcerned, as if she belonged in oak-panelled elevators. The woman glanced down at her, saw her left foot, and turned instantly away.

The lift opened on to a corridor. At one end were six marble steps, and an oak double door. The couple knocked, the door opened, there were shrill cries of delight, a burst of music leaked out, and they disappeared inside. From behind the door came the tail-ends of dozens of conversations. Sorrotore was indeed having a party.

'*Run,*' said every instinct in Vita's body. *I could come back another time*, she thought. Her stomach enthusiastically backed up the idea.

But her feet disagreed. Vita's feet were braver, at that moment, than the rest of her. They carried her up the five remaining steps, and her fist, the bravest of all, gave three short raps against the door.

The door opened immediately and a heavy-browed, white-gloved footman stood there with a professional smile. His black boots were so shiny they reflected a mirror image of his nostrils up at him.

His professional smile faltered at the sight in front of him. Vita fixed her eyes on him with disconcerting ferocity. Her cheeks, she could feel, were red with cold, and her jaw quivered, so tightly were her teeth set against each other.

'Yes? What do you want?'

Vita straightened her back, to gain a few inches. 'I would like to see Mr Sorrotore.' She tried to pronounce it as her grandfather had: 'Sorrow-tore-ae'.

'He's having a soirée – as you can see.' Behind and to the left, a double door opened on to the room Vita had seen. It was even larger than she had thought, and a cacophony of voices and laughter filtered through into the hall. 'Come back tomorrow.'

'Can you ask him, though, if he'll see me?'

'You want me to risk making him angry?'

Vita wondered, suddenly, if she should have kept back some of her money. Did footmen expect to be bribed?

'He might be just as angry if he finds out you sent me away. Tell him … my grandfather is Jack Welles.'

The footman looked hard at her. He pulled off a glove, and scratched his eye, the tip of his little finger brushing the eyeball. Then he sighed. 'If he's angry, I'll make sure it's you who deals with it.' He crossed into the brightly lit room. As he pulled the glove back on, Vita saw a tattoo, between his thumb and fore-finger, of a spitting cat.

Vita, left alone, stood waiting; then she pushed open the door into the drawing room, following the scent of perfume, sweat, and cigarette smoke.

It was like looking into a kaleidoscope. Couples dressed in bright colours danced in the centre of the room, or stood in groups around the edges, the women wearing diamonds large enough to kill a man, drinking hard and laughing loud. They wore splashes of rouge high on their cheekbones, and not one of them was not beautiful.

It was so hot the windows had misted over. But despite the heat, Vita wrapped her arms around herself and shivered: the laughter was too loud, as if covering over something: fear, or panic. The party seemed feverish, on edge. The women looked more like ornaments than flesh and blood. Alcohol, Vita knew, was illegal in New York under the law of Prohibition, and yet one woman sat staring at the wall, too drunk to stand.

A few noticed Vita, and she saw their eyes flick down to her ankle and their expression take on a familiar look of pity. She summoned her most unblinking glare, but she felt herself turning scarlet around the ears and neck.

She was edging back into the hall when one of the maids – a tall girl with a dirty white-blonde plait and a sharp, sullen face, barely older than Vita – said, '*Excuse me,*' and edged past her with a tray of champagne. Vita flattened herself against a wall, out of the way.

As Vita watched, a large white-haired man reached out to take the last champagne glass. He looked oddly familiar. The maid bobbed a curtsy and was moving back into the crowd with her empty tray when she stumbled over her own boot and brushed against the man. The girl's fingers flickered against his left wrist, and suddenly there was bare skin where his wristwatch had been.

Vita caught her breath. She was about to shout, to warn the man, when the girl caught her eye. She shook her head, once, urgently, and turned away, but not before Vita saw her expression. She looked like a cornered animal: trapped.

Vita was still hesitating when a voice spoke at her right ear.

'Are you the child asking for me?'

The man who addressed her did not look like his photograph, but she had no doubt at all that it was him.

'Yes,' she said. 'And you're Victor Sorrotore.'

He was taller than she had expected, and though his suit was exquisite, his nails were bitten right down to the quick, and bloody at the edges. His hair was carefully coated in brilliantine oil, but his eyes were shadowed by dark circles, as if someone had pressed two black inky thumbs against his face. The eyes fixed themselves on Vita's, and she felt the muscles in her chest contract.

'What is it you want?' he said. She hesitated for a moment, and he went on, 'I hope you didn't come all this way to tell me my own name?' His voice was deep, American, but accented with a European edge.

'I've come to ask you for something.'

'You interrupted my party to ask a favour?' He spoke as if to a much younger child. She stared back, and tried not to blink.

'It's business,' she said.

'Business! If it was business you wanted, why didn't you come during business hours?' He snorted, and there was cruelty in it. 'I would have offered you a cigar.' He looked her over, and she could see that he was performing some intricate, chilly calculation. 'Since you're here, let us go and find a desk and some leather furniture, so you feel sufficiently *businesslike*.'

He led the way. Out of the corner of her eye, Vita saw the maid with the waist-length plait make her way, stony-faced, among a group of laughing women. The diamond bracelet on one of their wrists disappeared.

Sorrotore stopped by the white-haired man, whose picture, she realised, she had seen in the American newspapers on the ship. A retired politician, she thought. Or, no: a retired Chief of Police. He was now a city developer and 'leading philanthropist', the papers had said, which sounded like a skin disease but presumably wasn't.

'Everything all right, Westerwicke?' said Sorrotore. 'Did it go as planned with Louie?'

Westerwicke nodded. 'I believe so. Right, Dillinger?' And he turned to a younger man standing at his elbow, with sparse sandy eyebrows and a sullen look. The man turned deep red, but nodded.

'I guess.'

'And the proof?' said Sorrotore.

Dillinger reached inside his breast pocket and pulled out a small brown envelope. He tipped a gold signet ring into his palm and held it out. 'Here.'

'Fine.' Sorrotore took it. 'I've got to deal with this –' he gestured at Vita – 'but I'll be right out.'

'Don't hurry on my account.' Westerwicke looked down at Vita and smiled: it was the smile of someone who does not like or trust children.

Sorrotore led her into a dark, wood-panelled room. The fire was smoking, and its scent was unfamiliar, as if he had doused the wood in perfume. Vita shook herself, hard, flexing her fingers inside her pockets; the party and the smoke together were making her feel dizzy, unmoored from herself.

A movement in the corner of the room made her jump.

'Don't mind the animals,' said Sorrotore.

She stared, as from behind a sofa came two tortoises, one as small as a side-plate, the other as large as a bicycle wheel. They moved cautiously, slowly, slipping a little on the polished wood. As they came closer, she saw with a jolt that they had gems set into their shells. The larger one had a word spelled out in sparkling white stones: 'IMPERIUM'. The smaller had a word spelled out in red. She saw with a shock that it said: 'VITA'.

'Rubies,' said Sorrotore. 'And the white ones are diamonds. Not particularly high quality carat, but I think they're rather charming. *Imperium* is Latin for "power". *Vita* –' and he gave a swift, hooded look – 'means "life". Power is life, life is power.' Vita's forehead creased. 'Only those who have power really live. I don't like to forget it. They help me remember.'

'Doesn't it hurt them?' asked Vita.

'Hurt them? Don't be crazy – they're animals.'

Two armchairs stood on either side of the fire. Sorrotore placed the signet ring on the mantelpiece and sat down in one chair, gesturing Vita to the other. She sank into it with relief; her foot was beginning to shake and burn.

'Now.' The jocularity had gone out of his voice. 'Tell me why you're here.'

'I'm the granddaughter of Jack Welles,' she said.

He sighed. 'Obviously I knew that, or you'd be down in the street by now.'

'I'm here to ask –' and Vita tried to make her voice sound tough-minded and official – 'to see the paperwork relating to my grandfather's home.' The words came out too high and thin.

The smaller tortoise nipped suddenly at the back of Sorrotore's heel. He gave a hiss of shock, and kicked his foot backwards, sending the tortoise skittering over the varnished floor. It bumped against a wall and landed on its back, its feet waving in the air.

'Your tortoise!' said Vita.

'What about it?'

Vita said nothing. She got up, crossed the room, trying to hide her limp from him, and set the tortoise the right way up. Sorrotore gave a bark of unamused laughter.

'I see I've got a little Saint Francis on my hands. What do you mean, you want to look at the paperwork?'

'I want you to prove that you bought Hudson Castle legally. I want you to show me.'

'*Prove?* You expect a grown man to engage in some ridiculous game at the order of a child?'

He did not meet her eyes as he spoke, and Vita felt her temper rise to match his. He was a cheat, underneath the brilliantined hair and the gold watch; she felt sure of it. 'You took my grandfather's house, and everything in it.'

'*Took* is not the right word. He sold it to me – cheaply, admittedly, but that was his choice. It's built, as you may or may not know, on an extremely rare and beautiful ornamental lake. I would be stupid not to take the opportunity.'

'No! He said he would rent it to you—'

'Are you accusing me of lying?'

The spit of the fire and the scent of the room made Vita want to retch. Her head was lurching from thought to thought. Desperately, through the growing mist in her mind, she tried a different tack. 'At least let him go back to pack his things. There's an emerald necklace, and if you don't let him fetch it, that's illegal—'

She tried to bite back the words. But he seemed to

have barely registered them. He stood and glanced in the mirror, rearranging the way his oiled hair fell across his forehead.

'This is a joke that I have no time for. I will show you out.'

'No!' She tried to summon herself back, to remember what she knew to be true. 'You're a thief!'

Sorrotore looked at Vita, and the look pushed her backwards against the armchair. 'What did you just say?'

'I said you're a thief,' said Vita, in a voice that was just above a whisper.

'How *dare* you?' he breathed.

His face was full of something like disgust. She had prepared herself for a denial, but not for such anger, and she felt herself straining not to cry.

'Do you know what happens to people who come to my apartment and accuse me of lying to my face?'

Before Vita could answer, there was a knock, and the butler put his head around the door. 'Mr Westerwicke is being called away, sir – he'd like to see you for a second before he leaves.'

Sorrotore swore, grunted, and strode out of the room without looking at Vita.

Vita's breath was hot in her chest, but she forced herself to stand. '*Get up,*' she whispered to herself. '*Don't be pathetic. This is what you came for. Reconnaissance. You've got to know the enemy. Look around. Something, anything, could be useful.*'

On the desk was a pile of papers, at least fifteen pages. She fumbled through them. At the top of each document were the words 'Deed of Sale'. All of the sums were $200 – astonishingly low. She noted, puzzled, that they were not addressed to Sorrotore, but to corporations with carefully boring names. She leafed through: Expedient Constructions was buying The Old Hotel on Columbus Avenue. North Manhattan Enterprises was purchasing a block of apartments of 'architectural significance' on East 23rd. The list was long.

She crossed to the mantelpiece, on which stood several invitation cards, and a photograph of a beautiful woman, signed '*Darling V! love, Lillian Gish*'.

She picked up the ring Sorrotore had set there; the gold disc, engraved with the initials 'LZ', glinted in the firelight. It was too large for any of her fingers, so she slipped it on to her thumb and held it out, to see it spark red and yellow.

There were footsteps in the room outside. She tugged at the ring. It stuck below the joint of her thumb. The doorknob twisted and Vita bit at the ring, trying to drag it off with her teeth. The door opened. Panicked, Vita shoved her left hand in her pocket, and darted to sit down again.

Sorrotore came back in, and this time his face was sad. 'Now, kid – listen to me. Glance around you. I imagine you noticed I'm a rich man.'

Vita did not need to glance. She knew the whole room looked like money.

'So why would I need to steal? Your grandfather said the Castle was a burden. He wanted to be free of it. I bought it. To be a canny businessman isn't a crime. It's mine, and I will not give it back; but nor –' and his eyes darkened – 'will I have it spread around town that I'm a common thief.'

'Grandfather swore he didn't! He wouldn't lie.'

'He lies because he regrets it. He lies because he's embarrassed. He lies because he feels like a foolish old man.' His voice became an intonation: a hypnotic, dark-voiced burr. 'He lies because he *is* a foolish old man.'

'He doesn't lie! I *know* him!' but an edge of doubt was creeping in; she could hear it, and flinched away from her own voice.

'You know, in your heart, that it's true. I think it would help you to say it out loud. Your grandfather lied.' And again, slower, 'Say, "My grandfather lied."'

'He *didn't!*'

'You've built a fantasy of wrong-doing and injustice around an old man's mistake. Admit it. Say, "My grandfather lied."'

Horror and embarrassment and something new, unidentifiable and unspeakable, flooded over Vita.

Renunciation, whispered the harsh, bitter little voice that lives in the dark depths of the heart. *Say he lied, and you won't need to worry any more. Poor foolish*

Grandpa. You can take him back to England. You can forget the plan. It's so simple.

Say it, and you'll be free.

The fire flickered, and Vita shrank further into her chair. She bit her lips together, holding back the words, and shook her head.

'It will help you, Vita. Say, "My grandfather lied."'

Vita's mouth opened to speak.

CHAPTER FIVE

Acrash loud enough to shake the floorboards
came from somewhere down the corridor.

Sorrotore jerked as if he'd been shot. He darted for
the door. People in the large party room were exclaiming
with pleased surprise at the unexpected drama.

'What was that noise?' called the woman with the
diamond-studded feather in her hair. 'It sounded like
smashing ice – did the little girl break your heart?'

The door to the study slammed shut, and Vita was
alone. She stood in the middle of the room. Her

upper lip was beaded with sweat, and she was breathing as if she had run miles.

Suddenly the sash window wrenched upwards, and a girl clambered in over the sill.

'Come on!' she said. 'Quick. This way.'

It was the blonde waitress.

Vita stared at her. 'What's going on?'

'Later. Out the window.' Her accent was not American but Irish, and perhaps a little English. 'Come on.'

'We're miles up!'

'*Come on!* Fire escape!'

Vita ran across the room. The window opened on to a metal balcony, with a long metal ladder leading to a platform below; which led, in turn, to more balconies, more ladders, and the ground.

Vita swung her leg over the edge of the sill.

'Faster.' The waitress spat on her palms and led the way down the first ladder, her hands and feet swift and confident. The final ladder did not reach the pavement; the girl hung by her hands for a second, and dropped. Vita, her hair blowing in her eyes, took hold of the ladder, counted to three, and fell. She tried to land on her right leg, but even so it sent agonising shock waves through her left foot, and she bent to rub at her ankle, ducking behind her hair to hide the pain.

'What was that crash? Was that you?' she said.

'Not here,' said the girl. 'Come on.'

They crossed the road and began walking away from the Dakota, mingling with the crowds.

Vita's left foot was throbbing at every step, and her patience was running thin. 'Tell me what happened!' she said. 'Now, or I'll shout.'

The girl sighed. 'I was listening outside the window.'

'Why?'

'Because you noticed me … working.'

'Stealing?'

'Working. And you didn't say anything. But I wanted to check – check you weren't ratting. So I listened. And all I could hear was that man, Sorrotore, trying to con you.'

'*Con* me?'

'Yeah. I know what a con artist sounds like.'

49

'How?'

The girl sounded surprised. 'Well, I am one.'

'I thought you were a pickpocket.'

'Both. And a lock-pick, too.'

'Really?'

They were passing a blue mailbox; the girl pulled a long sliver of metal from her stocking, bending over the lock on the front. 'Yes, really.' The box clicked open.

Vita glanced behind her. 'What are you doing?'

'Sometimes there's money in the envelopes. But that's dirty work, because you don't know who you're stealing from. I don't do that, not any more.'

'Close it!' said Vita. 'Someone will see!'

The girl kicked it closed. 'But I used to con for a living, when I was young. It was horrible – it's the worst job there is, worse than post-lifting, even – but I learned how to sound like Sorrotore did, how to sound hurt and wounded and patient and forgiving when I lied.' She glanced behind her, saw a car slow as it drove past, and pushed Vita down another road. 'Did you notice how he got angry? The best defence, when you've done something wrong, is anger.

'So I was outside the window, wondering why a grown adult's trying to put something over on a kid. And I thought I'd do something.'

'What did you do? What was the noise?'

'I spilt some red wine on my uniform, so's I'd have an excuse to go to the kitchen to get a cloth. Then I saw this room with this white china statue of that man, Sorrotore, in it – just his head – and it looked so handsome and noble that I wanted to kick it. I only gave it a tap, though – just so the wind could have done it – and it fell on the floor and smashed.'

'Ah,' said Vita.

'And then I crawled back on to your window sill and dragged you out.' She looked Vita up and down. 'So … what were you doing?'

'That man stole something from my family. I went to ask for it back.'

The girl stared at Vita. 'Ask for it back?' She snorted. 'Listen – and I say this speaking as a thief – that's insane. *Ask for it back!* You wouldn't last three minutes in the Bowery!' She seemed almost angry. 'You don't

51

know *anything* about the real world, do you? People like you are dangerous!'

'Like me?' Vita bristled.

'Stupid! Naive! *Hopeful!*' They turned a corner and the girl stopped abruptly. 'Not that way,' she said.

Two boys, a few years older than Vita, stood leaning against a doorway.

'Who are they?'

She turned on her heel. 'People I don't want to talk to.'

There was a shout, and two sets of running steps came after them. 'Hey! Hey, Silk!'

The girl made a rude gesture across the street. 'Ach, get out of it!' she called.

'Is that your name?' asked Vita. 'Silk?'

The taller of the boys began to run. 'Silk! Hey! Don't you walk away – you owe us! What you got from tonight?'

But Silk had darted across the road and disappeared among the crush. The boys followed, leaving Vita standing, her head whirling, on the dark pavement.

Vita thought of Silk's words: 'stupid', 'naive',

'hopeful'. She did not feel naive. She did not feel, precisely, hopeful: it was not hope that burned in her stomach and heart, but grim determination. And Vita was not stupid: she could feel the speed with which her mind spun and flashed. Her brain built things; plans, pictures, stories. Especially plans.

She pulled the map from her pocket and set off in pursuit, towards the Bowery.

There was trouble, when Vita returned, but Mama was exhausted, and Vita explained she had lost track of time exploring, and the lecture she received was not, overall, as furious as it might have been.

Vita retreated to her bedroom, and took out her red notebook. She saw again, with a thump of guilt, that she was still wearing the ring. She found some soap in the bathroom, coated her thumb in it and eased the ring off, hiding it in the pocket of her coat.

Then she filled her fountain pen with black ink, covering her fingers in the process. She bit down so hard on her lip it drew blood, and she began to write:

I found the girl outside a pawnbroker in the Bowery. She didn't want to listen, but I made her: I told her I'd go to the police if she didn't give me five minutes. I wasn't proud of that, but I did it. I needed to.

I said, 'I've got a plan. I need help. And I can pay you.'

I told her everything I know about Hudson Castle. I've never been, but I've heard Grandpa's stories a thousand times.

I told her about the lake, and how the house is built right in the middle of the water. I told her about the burglar bars, which my great-grandfather put on every window, after the robbery of 1888. He put in unpickable locks, too, on every door. Grandpa always called it 'the old fortress'. Nobody can get in. Nobody can get out.

And I told her the plan:

We're going to steal back Grandpa's emerald.

The Castle is impossible to break into. Luckily, we don't have to.

The emerald, Grandpa says, is hidden in the family's old hiding place. Which means under the paving slabs by the fountain in the walled rose garden.

There are two guard dogs. They bite. So I need someone to tame them.

She said, 'You could just kill them,' but I ignored her.

There's a wall around the whole garden. So I need someone to help me get over it.

And the rose garden, Grandpa says, has a door with a lock the size of your head. I need someone to pick it.

I need a team. We'd leave New York on a late-night train, so that it's dark. We would break into the garden, dig up the emerald, break out again, and be back at Grand Central Station before midday. Nobody will know we've been there.

And we'll sell the emerald, and get a lawyer, and get back the house, and Grandpa will have a home. And then he'll be able to breathe again.

Silk said no.

She had listened, her face clenched and sceptical, until Vita had finished. 'I don't have any money right now,' said Vita, 'but once we've sold the emerald, there would be enough to pay you a fee. A proper one.'

Then Silk shook her head. The look in her eyes was too old for a child.

'No. Even if it wasn't insane – which, incidentally, it absolutely is – I never work with anyone else. I don't do teams.'

'Never?'

'No. I've been asked before.'

'But if—'

'I don't care about buts or ifs. I can't get caught. Will you understand that? I *can't*. The police – they'd want to know who my guardian is, and then they'd work out I haven't got one, and then I'd be a ward of the state before you can say "But if".'

'This is different. I have a proper plan. Plans are the thing I'm good at.'

'You ever stolen anything before?'

'Well, no, not exactly—'

'*Exactly*. Every new person you work with is just another chance of getting caught. No.'

'What about those boys? I saw you with them—'

'I don't work *with* them. I owe them – or they say I do. Once I pay them off, I'm never doing any of that again: not pickpocketing, not lock-picking, not anything.'

'I know that! I could see – from your face – back at the party – I could see that it wasn't simple. But this is different – it's stealing *back*.'

'No.'

'Would you consider it if I said I've found a way that you couldn't possibly get caught – because I have! I swear.'

'No.' And Silk shifted away, her back an effective punctuation mark. 'Leave me alone.'

But Vita did not write that in her red book. Because she did not intend to take no for an answer.

CHAPTER SIX

Vita woke early the next morning, before the sun rose. It is difficult to sleep when you are besieged by hope. She ran her thumb along the paper edge of the red notebook.

She unpacked her binoculars from her suitcase: they had been her father's, and one eye was cracked, but she could use the other like a telescope. She crossed to the window and stared out, expecting to see a few people sleepily hauling themselves to work.

Instead, she saw a white horse. It was little more

than a speck, out on Seventh Avenue by the Park, galloping through the empty streets of the grey dawn-lit city, a boy riding bareback and coatless, his head ducked down against the bitter wind, laughing. A black bird flew overhead, keeping pace with him.

Vita leaned further out, focusing the one good eye of the binoculars. The boy's sweater was scarlet, and it shone, even in the dark. With a swoop to her chest, Vita recognised him: it was the boy from Carnegie Hall. Not the boy who had jumped, but the shorter, white boy. He rode leaning forwards, rear in the air, urging his horse on, his hair falling into his eyes. Vita had never seen a horse move so fast.

She didn't let herself stop to think about what was wise. Swiftly she dressed in her skirt, jersey, scarf, and boots, coaxing the left one over her foot, which still throbbed from the night before. She pulled on her ivory-coloured trench coat which had, once, belonged to her mother, taken in at the wrist and waist. She wrapped it around herself like armour, pushed the red book into her coat pocket, and stepped out into the city.

She was just in time to see the boy canter down

the street and come to an abrupt halt. He swung down to the pavement, and leaned in to whisper in the horse's ear. Then, as calmly as if he were escorting it in for a Bach piano concerto, he led the horse up the pavement towards the vast front doors of Carnegie Hall.

'Wait!' called Vita.

The boy whipped round with the speed of the guilty. His face was flushed, but when he saw who it was, he grinned.

'Oi! Don't *do* that! I thought you were my father!'

His accent was strong, and not English. *Spanish?* thought Vita. She crossed the road towards him. 'What are you doing?'

'Taking Moscow in,' he said.

Russian! she thought.

'She'll be hungry,' said the boy. He was not tall or broad, but when he grinned it was so vivid that he appeared to take up most of the street and at least half the sky. 'And we mustn't be caught.'

'Isn't she allowed to be in the street?'

'It's not that she's not allowed – she has to be

exercised twice a day – but I'm not supposed to be the one who does it. Samuel is. Also, I'm supposed to take her in the back way.'

Vita ran her hand down the horse's muzzle. It was soft as swan's down. 'Hello,' she whispered. 'I hadn't expected to see a thing as fine as you, not today.'

A gust of wind whipped Moscow's mane into the air, and the boy shivered. Vita pulled off her scarf and offered it to him. She expected him to politely refuse, but he took it with a grin and wrapped it round his neck.

'Thanks! What's your name?' But, contrary to the usual convention, he didn't stop to wait for an answer. 'I'm Arkady. I've seen you before, haven't I? When Samuel was trying the double-tuck spin out of the window?'

'I'm living opposite you for a couple of weeks. I'm Vita.' She stroked Moscow's heaving flank. 'Where does she live?'

Arkady grinned. 'Do you want to come and see?'

He didn't wait for a reply; he did not seem the kind of person who waited. He clicked his tongue at the horse, which shadowed him like a dog, and ran up the pavement to the Hall. Vita followed.

He pushed open one half of the huge double doors – 'I left it unlocked,' he said, 'but don't tell my father –' and Vita found herself in the reception of Carnegie Hall.

The sweeping staircase was wide enough to drive three elephants up it abreast – if you had had some elephants to hand. Its gilt banisters shone in the first morning light, and reflected gold up to the crystal chandeliers overhead. Ticket offices lined the far wall. Everything was impeccably clean. Vita looked at her nails and put her hands behind her back.

'This way,' said Arkady. 'I have to take Moscow to her stable, before I get caught.'

Their footsteps rang unnaturally loudly as they ran across the hall, Moscow clip-clopping after them. A large lift, with gleaming mahogany doors, stood open. Arkady led the horse inside. Vita followed.

'The stable … is in the lift?'

'Of course not. Third floor,' said Arkady, and pressed the button. They emerged and hurried down a long corridor. He seemed to notice Vita's stunned expression. 'Usually we tour with tents, and a special train car for the animals, but in the winters we try to find somewhere with a theatre. Some of the families rent flats. My mother and father, and a few others, we sleep above the theatre.'

Vita looked around with wonder. 'So ... you're performing at Carnegie Hall?'

'Of course! Every night at seven p.m. Not me, obviously – they won't let me until I'm fourteen – but my family.'

'How long have you been on tour?'

'Forever! Too long! Since I was a baby.' He seemed surprised. 'Haven't you heard of the Lazarenko Circus? Where do you live, in a cave? In a hole? In *Belgium*?'

'No! In England.'

'Ah,' he said, as if he considered all four roughly equivalent. He pushed open a door at the end of the corridor, and led the horse in. 'This is the Gold Ballroom. You can rent it for parties, after the opera.'

Dawn light struggled into the room. Along the

walls there were paintings of women with vertical hairstyles and men with horizontal moustaches. They seemed to thrum, as if they had captured some of the music of old.

Moscow trotted across the wooden floor to a space in the corner, where straw was piled high, and a trough of water stood. She began to drink, watched by a portrait of George Washington. The light caught her flank and cast it into pure silver.

'She's amazing—'

'Shh,' said Arkady. 'Wait.' And he whistled, and called out: '*Ko mne!*'

Before Vita could ask him to translate, something huge and roaring came hurtling out of the far corner.

It leaped straight at Arkady's face and Vita gasped, searching around her for something to throw.

The thing put both paws on Arkady's shoulders and began to try to lick the insides of his nostrils.

'This is Cork,' said Arkady. He pushed him away, laughing. 'Sit, Cork! He was a stray. I found him in the Park a few months ago and my parents let me take him in. At least, sort of. My mother did. Technically, my father doesn't know. He doesn't come in here.'

The dog was the size of a bear. His fur was blonde-white, and he was so huge that, even sitting, his head came up to Vita's ribs.

'What breed is he?' She held out her palm, rather warily, and the dog dipped his muzzle to her skin. His nose was very soft and wet, and gentle as a breath of air. She scratched behind his ears, and the dog let out a whine of pleasure.

'A mutt. All the best dogs are mutts. I'm pretty sure he's part Alsatian, and some Labrador. I think his father was a Caucasian Ovcharka. Watch!'

He made two fingers into a gun, and pointed them at the dog.

'Bang!'

Cork staggered backwards, collapsed on to his side, and let out a howl. Arkady laughed, and clapped once: the dog rose on to his hind legs and walked a few stately paces, his muzzle in the air. Then he rolled over and over, spun in a circle, marched backwards, and the boy barely had to move; Cork seemed to read his mind.

'He's brilliant! He's so clever!' said Vita. 'And he has the face of a king.'

Arkady gave her his sudden smile. 'I know. Most people are afraid of him, because—'

'Because he's big enough to eat a person and still have room for dessert?'

'Exactly! But he only ever bit me a little bit, when I first met him, and only because he was scared. And anyway most of the skin grew back. Stupid!' he said. 'But you're not stupid.' He looked hard at her, sweeping over her with his eyes, taking in her watching expression, the intensity of her gaze. 'So. In that case ...'

'In what case?'

'I can show you my secret.'

'The dog isn't your secret?'

'No!'

And he crossed to the vast window, threw it open, and whistled.

Vita's first impression was that they were being

attacked, and that their assailants had wings. She ducked as dozens of birds came skimming in through the window and filled the ballroom, landing on top of the paintings, drinking from the horse's trough, flocking round Arkady's head.

At first, most of the birds seemed brown, but as she looked, she saw the variation in their wings: the white speckling on the breast of the thrush, the pure white of the doves, the tropical orange of the black-birds' beaks.

'They know it's feeding time,' he said. 'They wait, in the trees nearby, every day.' He pulled handfuls of seed from his pockets, and almost disappeared beneath the storm of feathers.

'Here,' he said, 'take some,' and he poured seed into her hands. She found herself besieged by warmth, by sharp beaks and imperious feet and feathers beating against her cheek. Then the food was gone, and they abandoned her, returning to pick at the seed around Arkady's feet.

'Are they tame?' she asked.

'No. Not like you mean – not circus-tame. Mostly

it's only that they know me and I feed them.' Already some of the birds were leaving, the way they had come. 'But two of them are different.'

'Which?'

'The crows. I raised them from chicks. They're still young. One's over there, on the portrait of the constipated-looking Admiral. That's Rimsky.' His voice rang with pride as he said, 'She knows her name – they both do.'

'Really?' Vita had never heard of a bird knowing its name, and scepticism must have crept into her voice because Arkady scowled at her.

'Rimsky!' He made a whistling, hissing sound through his teeth. The crow took off, sweeping in three lazy flaps to land on Arkady's outstretched hand. She hopped up Arkady's arm to his elbow, leaned over to the boy's breast pocket, fished a crust from it, gave him a peck on the thumb, and took off again.

Arkady sucked a small amount of blood from his thumb. 'Bird affection takes a bit of getting used to. They're as clever as dogs, crows – they bring me presents from the street. Look!' He pulled a shining silver button from his pocket. 'Rimsky gave me this yesterday.'

'Where's the other one?'

'Rasko?' Arkady laughed. 'How would I know? Anywhere, in the whole city.'

'But you said they're tame.'

'Yes! But I didn't say he's my servant.'

A question was tugging at Vita. 'Why?' she asked. 'Feeding all those birds, taming the crows – Why?'

'One day, I'm going to have my own act. My family works with dogs – six poodles – and Mr Kawadza, he works with the horses. But I want more – I want a circus made from ... ach – there's an expression in Russian – it means, the hidden wilderness. You know? There's so much that's alive, even in the streets of the city, if you look for it. I want horses, because horses love to work – but also old mutts and crows – maybe squirrels – maybe mice, if I can work out how – all dancing to the same waltz together. Like a city turned into an animal ballet. Can you imagine?'

'It would be amazing.'

'But it's hard. After the revolution in my country, all the circuses were nationalised – there was nowhere in the whole of Russia we could have a theatre of our own, so we had to tour. Touring, touring, for nearly ten years! And every place, I get to know the birds, and then we move. I won't be able to take Rimsky and Rasko when we leave – they can't live in a cage. I want to stay still – I don't care where. But Papa says he'll either buy the perfect building or none at all – which I think is just his way of saying no.'

He turned to close the window, and as he did, a large rock came flying out of nowhere and struck him on the back of the head. Or … no, Vita saw. Not a rock: a crow.

'Rasko!' Arkady laughed. 'See! He's named after Raskolnikov – you know, the murderer? Like I said, the kindness of birds is a painful thing.'

He stood, a crow on each shoulder, the dog at his heels, the white mare watching him from across the floor. This, Vita thought, was how gold ballrooms should be used.

Arkady picked his nose and studied the snot. He

sighed. 'It's black,' he said. 'The city makes it black.'
Rimsky pecked at the snot on Arkady's finger. Arkady
looked at Vita. 'You'll keep this a secret?'

'Yes!' said Vita. The thought that had been prickling
at the back of her mind pushed itself forwards. Before
doubt could creep in, she forced herself to ask the
question. 'Can you keep one in return?'

She outlined her plan to Arkady, swiftly, while Rimsky
fluttered around them, pecking at her shoe. She
showed him the red book, pulling it from her coat
pocket and laying it on the floor between them.

Arkady did not, like Silk, say no; he did not even
say yes; he laughed until he choked and Rasko took
off in high dudgeon.

'I should have known! You, a thief!'

'It's not stealing if it's stealing back ...' began Vita,
but he wasn't listening.

He ran his fingers along her writing on the book:
THE PLAN. 'I knew there was something! So quiet,
but your face with that look – like you're always
watching – like you're thinking eight things at once.

71

Brilliant! *Otlichno!* Show me the book again? Emerald necklace, ancient house, train journey, break in, run away, yes?'

'Yes,' said Vita.

'Easy! What do you need me to do?'

'I can pay you,' said Vita. 'Not right now, but when we sell the emerald ...'

Arkady glared at her. 'I don't need money.' He thumped his chest. 'I will do it for the glory! We'll go down in history – like Robin Hood! The good thieves!'

'But I don't want you to think—'

'I *said*, what do you need?'

'I need to get over a wall – a high wall, in the middle of the night. And there're two guard dogs. They've been trained to kill. Can you help?'

'The dogs, yes! Wonderful! All dogs, all the time! The wall – how high?'

'I don't know. Maybe fifteen feet – maybe twenty? Or more?'

Arkady was suddenly serious. 'For that, no. I'm not a climber. For that, you need someone else.'

'Who?'

72

'You need Samuel. Samuel Kawadza. He can fly.'

Far in the recesses of the building, a door slammed, and there was the sharp hoot of a tin whistle.

Arkady jumped. 'My father's awake. You need to go. Come back tonight!' he said. 'For Samuel!'

'When? And what do you mean, fly?'

'Too many questions! I don't know – whenever everyone else is asleep.' Arkady pulled her to the window, and pointed. 'You can jump out.'

Vita peered down. The breakfast traffic below was already bustling.

'Wouldn't I break my leg?'

'Only a small one, maybe.'

Vita looked down at her red shoes. Arkady's gaze followed hers, to the shape of her shoe, the thick sole, the way her leg bowed outwards.

'Actually,' he said, 'I'd take the elevator. Why walk when you can ride? Come!'

'You don't need to come with me. I remember the way.'

'Fine – quick, then. Have this.' Arkady reached into his pocket and thrust a handful of birdseed into

Vita's fist. 'Put it on your window sill after dark and wait – I'll send Rasko to get you when it's time!'

And soon Vita found herself on the street, the morning growing swift around her, looking up at the Hall. Nothing had changed, and yet it looked entirely different, now she knew it stored horses in the ballroom.

As Vita crossed the road back to the apartment building, she saw the paperboy, barking the *New York Times* headlines.

'Cyclone Louie shot dead in a diner! Louie Zwerback dead!'

Vita's forehead prickled, and adrenaline jerked through her fingers; she was afraid before she knew why she should be. She searched in her coat pocket for two cents, took a paper, and read it on the street corner.

'*Louie Zwerback, a notorious Brooklyn smuggler, has been gunned down as he drank coffee in an all-night diner. More on page 3.*'

Vita wrestled to turn to page three, the paper flapping in the wind.

'The hit on Zwerback appeared to be a simple job gone wrong; several people were injured, and the assassins, who covered their faces, fled after stripping Louie of his signet ring.'

Vita's chest was solid ice. She felt inside the pocket of her red skirt and took out the ring. She looked at the initials, *LZ*, stamped on the gold disc. Her first instinct was to throw it down the grate of the storm drain. But a voice in her head jerked her hand back: *Evidence.* She stopped herself and pushed it deep inside the pocket of her skirt.

She thought of Westerwicke's laughing face, and Sorrotore's fireside words. '*Do you know what happens to people who come to my apartment and accuse me of lying to my face?*'

Vita wrapped her coat more tightly around her body. The ache in her foot was growing vivid, and she felt suddenly small, barely big enough to breathe, in a large and adult world.

CHAPTER SEVEN

Vita let herself into the apartment, twisting the doorknob as carefully as if it were glass. She'd been gone for far longer than she intended; her mother would already have left to meet Grandpa's bank manager, and Vita prayed her absence from her bed had not been noticed. She smelt slightly of horse, and bird, and her cheeks were flushed.

The apartment was silent. She tiptoed to her bedroom and pushed the ring under the bed; then hesitated, her arm still deep under the mattress.

What if Sorrotore found out where she lived? She took a needle and thread, unpicked an inch of the hem of her skirt, and tucked the ring inside, sewing it tightly to the lining. She was just biting off the thread when Grandpa knocked.

'Are you awake?'

Vita opened the door, and saw her grandfather wrapped in his green woollen coat. It looked far too big for him now, but he was smiling, and the spark was still in his eyes.

'Put this on, Rapscallion,' and he handed her his red woollen scarf. 'I've been inside too long. We're going to the Park.'

The leaves in Central Park were a bright, stark red against the blue of the sky, and coated the ground like a carpet. They followed the paved pathways, down winding tree-lined trails, Grandpa swinging his stick. A black woman dressed in an ankle-length coat went briskly past, pushing a cart selling hot chocolate. Grandpa saw Vita's imploring face, and gave her a coin.

'Get yourself the largest and thickest hot chocolate she has.' He creaked down on to a bench. 'I shall wait here, and commune with the squirrels.'

Vita went, as fast as she could, down the twisting tree-lined path. It forked; the woman was nowhere in sight, so she turned left, on to the wider avenue. Her limp was worse than usual, but the chocolate was beckoning.

The man came out of nowhere, rounding the corner.

'Hey! Hey! You!'

Vita froze. He was broad-shouldered and sandy-haired, and much younger than she had thought he was at the party. His eyes were pale grey, and they darted over her feet and leg, her red-brown hair. *Dillinger*, she thought.

'You were that kid at Sorrotore's party!' His voice was high, with a rasp to it that suggested cigarettes and alcohol.

Vita tried to look unafraid. 'What if I was?'

'What have you done with it?'

'Done with what?'

'The ring, you little brat! Where's the ring?' He slurred on the word 'where's', and she wondered whether it was anger or early morning drink.

Vita tried to keep her face and body utterly still. Only her heart defied her. 'What ring?' she said.

'Don't be cute, kid. Sorrotore tore the study apart looking for that ring. There's nobody else who could've taken it.' His clothes were loud and expensive, but had the rumpled look of someone who had not yet gone to bed. His silver wristwatch had not been wound, and pointed to midnight.

'I honestly don't know what you're talking about.' The ring, inside the sewn-up hem of her skirt, was pressing against her leg.

'Listen, kid.' He leaned down, his face close to hers. 'You don't know what you're dealing with. Things aren't so good for the boss right now. He's unpredictable. Hand it over, and he'll forget it.'

'I don't have any ring! I don't know what you're talking about.' It was broad daylight, but the path had taken her out of Grandpa's view, and there was nobody in sight. She wondered if he would hear her scream. And what if he did hear, but couldn't help? The thought made her bite her lips together.

He grabbed her upper arm. 'So you won't mind me searching you, I guess?'

'Let go of me!'

A sudden something flew out of the air and struck the man on the shoulder. Vita looked down; it was a rock, as large as her palm.

'Step away!' Grandpa came striding down the pathway, leaning on his stick, his eyes ice cold. His voice as he reached them, though, was steady. 'I would be grateful if you'd explain what the hell you think you're doing touching my granddaughter?'

Dillinger stepped backwards, but kept his eyes on Vita. 'I wasn't doing anything. This kid of yours stole something from my boss.'

Grandpa moved in front of Vita, shielding her from the man. 'And who would your boss be?'

'Victor Sorrotore.'

Grandpa's eyes glanced round at Vita, but he remained facing Dillinger. 'I find it incredibly unlikely that my granddaughter would steal anything. And since your employer has stolen my entire home, I would say that if by some extraordinary chance she has, he is scarcely in a position to complain.'

'Make her turn out her pockets!'

'You're ridiculous,' said Grandpa. 'Leave, now, or I'll shout for the police.'

Dillinger reached into his jacket. 'I wouldn't do that, you know,' he said.

When his hand came out, it held a small pistol. He did not point it at them, but dangled it loose in his hand.

Vita froze, staring at the gun. The barrel was barely bigger than her thumbnail, and yet it looked large enough to eclipse the sun. Dillinger handled it with the ease of a man who was accustomed to using a weapon to make a point.

Grandpa's eyes widened with shock, then narrowed with rage. 'Police!' he roared, his old voice lifting above the trees. 'Police! Help!'

'You senile old fool.' Dillinger was stumbling backwards, nostrils flaring. 'You don't know what you're doing! You're playing with fire, kid.' And he ran. The path forked, one broad and one narrow, and he darted down the narrow path. In the centre was a manhole and, through the trees, Vita watched in astonishment as he hauled up the cover, and dropped down into the darkness below.

'He went into the *sewer!*' she said, but Grandpa had not seen: his eyes were on her face, and he seemed uninterested in anything else.

'Do you want to explain what's going on? You went to see Sorrotore?'

Vita hesitated; then nodded.

Grandpa's eyes were dark. 'Why? Why would you do a thing so obviously, criminally, stupidly dangerous?'

'I just … Nothing happened. I wanted to see what he looked like.'

'And have you seen, now?' Grandfather's voice was tight. 'Have you seen what kind of man he is?'

Slowly, looking down at her left foot, Vita nodded.

'Will you promise not to go looking for him again? Ever? Promise, or I can never let you go out alone.'

'Yes,' she said. It wasn't a lie, she told herself. It was not Sorrotore she was looking for. And if he was looking for her, that was something very different. She had made no promise there.

Grandpa gave a great sigh, and he turned to sit on a tree stump at the edge of the path. His face was white, and though there was still fury in his eyes, it was directed inwards. 'Oh, my love. What have I done? I've put you in the way of such ugliness.'

'You haven't! Truly. I swear, I'll be careful.'

With one hand, she reached out and took Grandpa's hand. With the other, she reached into her pocket and felt for the red book. She rolled it up into a tube and clenched her fingers around it. She held her plan in her fist: a weapon, of sorts.

CHAPTER EIGHT

Vita waited until the sun had fully set before she
scattered the birdseed on the inside window
sill. The day birds had all gone to roost, and no
pigeons came to peck at it.

She sat next to it and waited; and waited. She was
almost asleep when there was a flurry of wings and of
bright eyes, and a crow landed on her window sill and
began to devour the seed.

The bird had a tiny roll of paper tied to its foot.

Taking a letter off a bird's foot is infinitely harder,

Vita discovered, than it is made to sound in books. The bird flapped round and round her room with Vita in gently urgent pursuit, and it was not until she thought to offer it the ginger snap she had been saving that it stayed still long enough for her to unwind the three wraps of string that held it in place.

The note read: '*Come to the entrance of Carnegie Hall at 11.20 p.m. Don't be even a minute late. Eat this note.*'

Vita looked at the note, which had suffered somewhat from its proximity to the bird's rear end, and decided not to eat it. She flushed it down the lavatory instead.

Arkady was waiting behind one of the front doors of the Hall, watching through a crack, and he pulled it open before she could wonder whether to knock.

'Come! A night guard patrols, but he only does the ground floor. He's just gone past. Quickly!'

He led Vita through the great hall, lit only by the street lamps outside, and into the lift. 'Second floor,' he said. 'The Chapter Hall.'

'The what?'

'It's like a tiny stage: just two hundred people. The main hall takes nearly three thousand. There's a rig in the Chapter.'

'What kind of rig?'

'Trapeze, obviously!' He looked shocked at her ignorance. 'The rig belongs to the Sabatini Sisters, but they don't mind Samuel using it. Or at least, they wouldn't mind if they knew. It has to be secret.'

'What does?'

'Samuel! He's training to be an acrobat.'

'Why does it have to be secret?'

'Because he comes from a horse family.' He shook his head at her, as if this were obvious. 'He has to join his uncle's act. It's why he's here – to learn horsemanship.'

'But couldn't he just ask—'

'No. Circus families work like royalty – you do what your parents did, by birthright. You get no more choice about it than Tsar Alexander had about being Tsar. Which is OK for me – I've always known I wanted to work with animals: with dogs and horses and birds.'

Vita thought of how his face had shone, bright as torchlight, as he rode Moscow across the sleeping city, and nodded.

'But the problem is, Samuel is a great aerial artiste,' said Arkady. She smiled at the word 'artiste', but his face was utterly serious. 'He taught himself, by watching – like people teach themselves tunes on a piano, you know? Except on his own body, and now he can't unlearn it. So.'

'But that's not fair!' said Vita.

Arkady shrugged. 'I know. But have you tried saying that to an adult recently?'

'That doesn't mean you can't change it. Nothing's unchangeable!'

But Arkady was running ahead. 'Come – here!'

The room was wooden-floored with wood panelling and a high ceiling. Chairs were laid out along three sides of the room, a single lamp was lit. The room smelt of sweat and chalk.

In the middle of the room were what looked like four rugby goal posts. Attached to the two posts at either end were platforms; from the middle two hung

87

what looked like small iron swings. Beneath them was a net. At the top of one platform was a boy, standing on one leg, the other held high above his head.

'Samuel!' called Arkady. 'She's here.'

The boy turned, and grinned, but went immediately back to his stretching; and Vita quietly reminded herself to blink.

Samuel was beautiful; and his beauty was of the kind that makes your lungs temporarily forget their function. He was clad entirely in black – black cotton trousers, a black singlet, black bands at his wrist, black ballet shoes. His hair was cropped close to his head, and his cheekbones slanted across his face like twin cliff-edges. He set both hands on the platform and kicked himself into a handstand.

'Talk now or later?' asked Arkady.

'Later,' said Samuel, upside down. He barely seemed to have registered Vita's presence. 'I'm trying something new.' His accent was New York, but with something else: a length and depth to the vowels that suggested a different mother tongue.

Samuel flipped upright, dipped his hands in chalk,

picked up a long pole with a crook at the end of it, and, leaning out over the edge of the platform, used it to draw the iron swing towards him. He caught hold of it with one hand, leaning out over the net with just his heels on the platform.

He looked down at Arkady, and his face was rigid with concentration.

'Call me in?' he said.

Arkady shouted back, '*Listo!*'

'*Listo?*' whispered Vita.

'Spanish for "ready".'

Samuel shifted his weight. 'Ready!'

'*Hep!*' called Arkady.

And Samuel cast himself off into the air, both hands on the bar of the trapeze, flying. At the peak of the swing, he let go, somersaulted in the air above the bar, and hooked back on to it with his knees. Vita's stomach lurched.

The boy spun upright, grasped the ropes on either side of the swing, and stood up on the bar. He swayed his body back and forth, and the swing soared, so high that at its peak he was facing directly downwards and Vita caught a fleeting glimpse of his face. Then, without the slightest noise, he let go and dropped forward, spinning a full circle in the air, up and over the swing with only his ankle hooked over the bar.

Vita gasped. It wasn't just the way he dropped through the air, as if gravity had granted him a special dispensation; it wasn't just his flight. It was the look that had transformed his face.

Samuel's jaw was set, and he did not smile, but there was something strange and prodigious and ferocious on his countenance. It was the joy of someone doing the thing they were born to do.

Vita did not know for how long Samuel swung, and spun, and cast his body kaleidoscope-wise. She only knew that she didn't want him to stop. Then, as the swing rose higher and higher, he let go and spun in a double somersault, falling as the swing fell, reached out to grab it, missed, and fell into the net.

He sat up, his eyes shining.

'New trick?' called Arkady.

'Didn't work,' said Samuel, standing in the net and brushing off his hands. 'Did you see what went wrong?'

Up close he was slight and lean, but with large hands and feet that said he would be tall, some day.

'You were on the downswing,' said Arkady. 'I think maybe two-thirds of a second too late,' he said. 'But I don't know if it's possible to do a double somersault.'

'It is!' Samuel shook his head. 'But I could feel I was off.' He jumped down from the net, wiping his forehead with his shirt. His flight had changed him; his whole body was looser, less wary.

'You're Vita,' he said. 'Ark said you need something.'

Vita felt for the red book in her pocket and gripped it tight. She straightened her spine. 'I need a team,' she said. And as swiftly as she could, she explained: about the Castle, and the emerald pendant, and the need for money and armies of lawyers to bring Sorrotore to his knees.

'I need to get over a wall, maybe fifteen or twenty feet.'

'Why can't you just take a ladder?'

'Because the wall rises straight out of a lake. A small one, but still a lake. It needs a rope.'

91

'A *lake*?' said Samuel.

'A *real* new trick!' said Arkady. His enthusiasm made his words pile up against one another. 'We're going to be thieves!'

Samuel frowned.

'No, I know what you're thinking,' said Arkady hurriedly, 'but it's stealing back what was already stolen. Good thieves!'

'Necessary thieves,' said Vita.

'And it's out in the countryside,' said Arkady, 'way out in nowhere, so we won't get caught. Probably, anyway.'

Samuel did not look convinced. 'Why, though? Why are you doing it?'

Vita looked up at the trapeze, which still swung back and forth above their heads.

'Because nobody else is going to do it,' she said.

'That's not actually a reason,' said Samuel. 'You could say that about almost anything.'

Vita bit her lip. 'Mama says we have to be sensible. She wants to make my grandfather come back home to England with us, whether he wants to or not. And Grandpa goes blank if you try to ask him about it. His whole face is like a door slamming shut.'

Vita closed her eyes, to hide from the thought – and then opened them.

'But if we just pack up and go home, Sorrotore will have won. He'll win, just like men like him always win. So I don't want to be sensible.'

She looked down at her left shoe, at the twist and arch of her foot, at the breakable thinness of her left leg. She thought of all the well-meaning adults, with their *sit-down, take-care, not-you-dears*. She shook her head, and straightened every bone in her body. 'Just once, I don't want to do what I'm told! I want to fight. I'm *going* to fight.'

Samuel looked at her for a long, thickly laden moment. 'My father's at home in Mashonaland, in Africa,' he said. 'He gave everything he had to send me out here, when I was a tiny kid, to tour with my uncle: to join the act. If I don't, I'm letting down the whole family: cousins, aunts: everyone. But – when I was three, I taught myself to backflip. I loved the way it felt when I landed back up on my feet: like a magic trick. I can't give it up.' He stared at his hands, which were covered in chalk. 'So – I can understand not wanting to do what you're told.'

And then he smiled, and the smile rose up to his ears and his disconcerting beauty vanished in favour of glee: the glee of the usually careful turned reckless. 'Exactly how wide is the wall?'

'I don't know. Quite wide, I think.'

'And exactly how tall?'

Vita shook her head. 'About fifteen feet. Maybe twenty. I don't know.'

'I need to know exactly. For the rope. Do you have a blueprint?'

'A what?' said Arkady. 'I don't know that word.'

'It's an architectural plan of a house,' said Samuel.

'I don't have one,' said Vita, 'but I can find one.' Her voice, she noted with relief, sounded far more confident than she felt.

'If you find one,' said Samuel, 'then I'm in. I'll join your heist.' And he wiped his chalky palms on his black trousers and stuck out his hand.

Arkady clapped his hands above his head and whooped, but an unexpected surge of hot guilt rose up in Vita's chest. The two boys stood, shoulder to shoulder, identical grins. They had never seen Sorrotore, nor seen the ice in him. She had not told them about the newspaper headline.

She pushed the guilt down, down where she could not feel it. She laid her hand in Samuel's and shook it.

'When do we go?' asked Arkady. 'Soon! Tomorrow!'

'Soon,' said Vita. 'But not tomorrow.'

'But why not tomorrow?'

'There's still a lot to do,' said Vita. 'Like Samuel says – every heist needs a blueprint.'

CHAPTER NINE

The next morning, Vita's mother left early again, walking across town to meet a series of grey-suited men who were sorting through Grandpa's tax and banking affairs. Grandpa read by the window. And Vita, moving silently through his bedroom, barefoot, searched every drawer and cupboard, looking for papers.

There was nothing. She should have realised, she told herself fiercely. '*Stupid*,' she whispered. She knew Grandpa had had to leave Hudson Castle with only the clothes he stood up in. Even so, it was a blow to the chest.

In the end, she did the simplest and most risky thing: she asked him.

'Blueprint? Of course there was.' He looked her up and down, his eyes sceptical. 'Why the interest? Your mother's right, Rapscallion – it's better to put all that behind us, now.'

'I just … wondered.'

'Wondered?' His tone was dry.

'It's for …' And Vita bit down, hard, on the inside of her cheeks before she lied. 'It's for a game. Where is it? Is it back in the Castle?'

'It's in the New York Public Library. We donated it, with a lot of other papers, many years ago. They sent out requests to all the old houses.'

'So I could see it?' Her heart rose.

'Would you like to tell me why?' He lifted first one eyebrow, then the other.

'No, thank you,' said Vita.

'It's better you forget it ever existed, Rapscallion.'

'No, thank you,' she said again.

And as she looked up at him, unblinking, he gave a great bark of laughter, loud as a bear atop a church tower.

'Your grandmother was stubborn too. It runs in the blood. Let me get my hat.'

His hat was moth-eaten, a black so faded it was closer to brown, but Grandpa had always worn his clothes with flair, and he set it on his head like a crown. The city was winter-sharp, and on the corner of West 47th Street, Grandpa stopped to buy a paper cone of sweet roasted peanuts.

Across the road, a white man in a black suit looked up and saw an old man with fine hands and a girl with red-brown hair and wide-set eyes. Her trench coat was wrapped tight over bright red boots and her left leg bowed inwards. His head jerked backwards. He put down the pretzel he was buying and set off after them, following half a block behind down the broad pavement.

By the time they reached the library, Vita's fingers were covered in hot syrup. She licked them thoroughly, looking up at the building across the road.

The building looked more like a palace than a library. Its pillars and portico stood, regal, as the colour and noise of the city swept by.

'This is my favourite place in New York,' said Grandfather. 'The lions are called Patience and Fortitude – though I always think they look furious, which I rather like.'

The lions did, in fact, look irate: two scowling white marble statues, guarding the city's books. Vita nodded at them as they made their way up the steps. They went arm in arm, she placing her left foot carefully on the broad stone, he with his stick, both with their eyes set on the wide welcoming doors.

The man in the black suit did not follow them inside. He stood, leaning up against a lion, waiting, blowing on his fingers. On the back of his hand was a tattoo of a spitting cat.

The librarian on duty was a Miss Sutton, a tall Latina woman dressed in velvet who greeted Grandpa like an old friend. She led the two of them down the long hall to a room flanked with desks and reading lights and scholars bent low over books.

'I'll put you down here,' she said, 'so you can talk without disturbing our other patrons.'

And she led them into a small room, containing one large leather-topped desk, several pairs of white gloves, and a green glass lamp that Vita immediately longed to touch.

Miss Sutton produced a box, its lid tied down with a string fastening, and left them. Vita lifted out the sheaf of papers, and sat down next to her grandfather. At the top was a sheet of paper, folded into eighths.

Grandpa spread it out on the desk.

'There!' he said, and his voice was less steady than before.

The paper was large, as big as an atlas, and so thin as to be almost transparent. But she could see that her grandfather was looking beyond the paper, into the house itself; allowing himself, just for this moment, to remember.

'It's older than the Constitution, the Castle – my great-grandfather brought it over by boat. Mad, of course, but who's to say that madness is so bad a thing? When my father died and we first moved there, before your mother was born, it was crumbling – the white walls moulding on the inside. So we painted the interior blue.'

Vita knew, of course, from the old stories. But even so, to make him talk, to keep that look in his eyes, she found herself saying, 'What kind of blue?'

'Jewel colours. Your grandma chose them. Bright cobalt blue, sapphire blue, turquoise. It used to shine.'

He pointed to the paper.

'There's the entrance hall. The old chandelier's still there, unless that man has taken it. There's the state staircase. Half-rotten, now, and liable to fall down at any second. We always took the back stairs. The cellar. My father's wine is still in it, unless Sorrotore's drunk it. That space in the back wall, you see – marked in black – that used to be the plumbing, but now it's just a grate. It ventilates the cellar, and ensures you can freeze your teeth off down there all year round.'

'And this?'

'That's the main sitting room. There was an old

stuffed polar bear rug – poor thing, your great-great-grandfather shot it, a man with very few brains but many, many guns. I used to lie next to it as a boy. The teeth used to keep coming out. It guards the safe – which is here, inside the chimney.'

'And see – front door. Back door. Unbreakable locks. Burglar bars. Your great-grandfather was convinced people were trying to steal his wealth. The rich are often paranoid and afraid. These days, of course, there is no wealth to steal.'

Vita looked at the drawing in silence. The walls around the castle were neatly labelled in beautiful architect's print. Nineteen feet high, and two feet wide.

'It's strange, to see it here on paper. I had vowed to forget it. I don't suppose I shall ever see it again.' He smiled and shook the long-lost look from his eyes. 'Now. Since we appear to have come, inadvertently, on a jaunt, shall we follow through? We could go in search of ice cream?'

Vita shook her head. 'I'd actually like to stay here. I'd like to copy it.'

Grandpa's eyebrows hitched upwards. 'Copy it?'

'It's for the game.'

'Do you care to tell me what game?'

Vita did not care to. She shook her head, hard.

Grandpa considered her; his red-booted, lion-eyed girl.

He sighed. 'Don't think, even for one second, that I don't know that you're lying,' he said. 'But I don't think children should be forbidden to have secrets. Only, can you promise me that this secret has nothing to do with Sorrotore?' Vita's heart sank, and she was wondering if she could lie to him when he added, 'Can you promise me, again, you'll go nowhere near him?'

Vita smiled, the sixth of her six smiles. 'I promise I won't go near Sorrotore.' She still had no intention of going near him.

'Good. Then I only ask that you respect my trust, by not getting killed, maimed, or arrested. I'll see you back at the apartment. Be home before your mother comes back, or she'll have every right to slaughter us both.'

*

Vita worked fast. It was only half an hour before she left the library and began the walk home, under the watchful eyes of the skyscrapers. Children walking alone in New York were not at all unusual, but even so, she drew looks, so fiercely did her eyes burn with purpose: she did not seem to see the great yellow and grey stone city around her, the shining lights, for her eyes were focused on some other, unseen point.

And the man with the cat tattoo left his post by Patience, and followed her down the street.

CHAPTER TEN

Vita spent the afternoon memorising the city. She walked, first home, for toast with ketchup. Grandpa was preparing to sleep, upright in a chair in his bedroom. 'The night,' he had said, when Vita asked, 'is become something of a giant. I seem unable to defeat it. But I sleep in snatches during the day, and that's more than enough for me.'

Then Vita walked, slowly, painfully, across half of Manhattan; over 57th Street, and down Fifth Avenue towards Madison Square Park. She was trying to fix her paper map of New York in her head: just in case. There was no telling, she thought, when it might be useful.

She returned to the apartment at tea-time, and let herself in as silently as possible. She did not call out, in case her grandfather was still asleep. Nothing seemed amiss until she reached her bedroom; and then the hairs rose on the back of her neck like a cornered cat.

Someone had been in her room.

Nothing had been ransacked – everything was impeccably neat – but her book was in a different place on the window sill, and her bed had been unmade and remade, with the blanket the wrong way up. Panic wrapped around her, and she threw open the wardrobe; there was nobody there, only her neatly folded jerseys and stockings. She looked under the bed. Nothing; except … the dust had been swept away, as if by a groping hand.

She ran to check the kitchen, the drawing room. There was so little furniture that it was almost impossible to tell, but someone had been there, soft-footed and silent. Vita thought of the ring, secure inside the hem of her skirt, and felt her heart pound in her ears.

She should go to the police; she should tell someone. But Westerwicke *was* the police: even though he was retired, it was too enormous a risk. And if she told her mother, she would change their tickets for the first boat home. Which left Grandpa. She tried to picture telling him, and knew, immediately, from the shooting pain in her chest, that Grandpa mustn't know. He would blame himself, and that was unthinkable.

Vita crossed to the kitchen and got out the ketchup bottle. She ate a spoonful, to give herself sugar, and courage. She would ask her mother to double-lock the door at night, and she would tell no one. And, in the meantime, she had a date with the circus.

It had all started quietly enough; legally enough, even. Vita had mentioned, the previous night under the moonlit trapeze, that she had never actually seen a circus.

The two boys looked at her, then at each other. It was as if she had said she had never seen the sky.

'You don't really mean it?' said Samuel. 'You don't mean it *literally*?'

'How could I have metaphorically not seen a circus?'

'Right,' said Arkady. There was an edge of panic in his voice. 'We have to fix this! Tomorrow night – there's a show at seven!'

'Wonderful!' said Vita, but she hesitated. Nothing about the shine and glow of Carnegie Hall suggested it would be cheap. 'How ... much will it be?'

'Don't be ridiculous,' said Samuel. 'We'll sneak you in.'

Vita's mother was still not home when Vita crept out of the apartment that night. She left a note, saying she was going to the circus – she did not say with whom – and would be back by bedtime. She knew there would be fury on her return, but that was then, and this was now, and this was the circus.

The two boys stood under the flag, waiting. A

young man was handing out leaflets; a single sheet, printed with a newspaper article. 'Rave reviews!' he called. 'Read our rave reviews in the *New York Times!*'

Samuel beckoned the boy over, took one, and handed it to Vita. 'Here,' he said in greeting. 'Souvenir.'

She read it out loud. '*Circus in Carnegie Hall! Elephants, ponies, dogs, and other familiar attractions of the tanbark …*' She broke off. 'What's a tanbark?'

'Small pieces of bark,' said Samuel. 'You know – the stuff they use to cover the floor of the circus ring.'

Vita kept reading. '*– of the tanbark, will be seen in Carnegie Hall this season with the presentation there of a genuine indoor circus.*'

'Good, no?' said Arkady. 'The *New York Times*! Papa was so happy he framed it and put one in every room – even the toilet.'

'Let's go,' said Samuel.

Vita pushed the leaflet into her pocket and stepped towards the main entrance, but Arkady gave a bark of laughter.

'Not that way!' he said. 'We have to go in the stage door.'

'What?'

'Well, we don't have tickets! We don't get them free – who do you think we are, Rockefellers?'

Samuel led the way around the corner to the side of the building.

'Did you get the blueprint?' he asked, as he nodded at the doorman.

'Yes,' said Vita. 'I copied it into my book.'

'Good,' he said, 'you can show us after the show,' and he led her up a flight of steep stairs. They made no mention of her foot, but, near the top, Samuel offered her his hand. She grinned at him but did not take it.

At the top of the stairs was a door in green baize. Samuel stood back. 'After you.'

Vita pushed the door open, and found herself in another country.

The lights were bright, and the air smelt of perfume, and chalk, and hot human bodies. A young Japanese woman stood on her hands in the corridor, scratching the back of her head with a toe. Everywhere people hurried to and fro, squeezing past each other;

every face was painted, and every person was clothed in a riot of exquisite silk and sequins.

Three women wearing leotards moved Arkady bodily aside, laughing in what Vita thought was Spanish.

'This way,' said Samuel.

Vita wanted to stop and stare, and stare, but Arkady caught hold of her hand and pulled her towards a high-ceilinged dark space.

'Here!' said Arkady, triumphant. Carnegie Hall, Vita saw, did not have wings like a traditional circus; instead, a wide door on each side led out on to the stage. Arkady pointed. 'We stand here, just by the door! We'll be able to see everything!'

A voice, Russian-accented, came from behind them. 'Arkady! What are you doing here?' A tall man with a bulbous nose glared down at them. 'Didn't I tell you last time, boys, you're blocking the way?'

'We just want to watch,' said Samuel softly.

'Who's this?' The man jerked an eyebrow at Vita.

'She's my friend.' Arkady was turning red. 'Vita, this is my uncle. He's the acting stage manager. She's never seen a circus, Uncle Yvgeny!'

'I can't have you …' he began, but then he saw Vita's face. Her eyes, looking about her, were hot with wonder. His eyes flickered down to her foot.

'I see,' he said, more gently. He dragged three chairs over and positioned them just outside the door. Vita smiled the third of her six smiles. 'Here. Sit still in these, don't make noise, and it'll probably be OK.'

The lights were beginning to dim, and the young woman from the corridor came and stood just outside the door. She rubbed the back of her neck, and winked at Vita.

'That's Maiko,' said Samuel. 'She's the lead tumbler.' His voice was full of awe. 'She trained with Nikitin himself.'

A man, dark-haired and long-legged, in a top hat and a black dinner jacket, strode on to the stage and addressed the audience.

'That's my father,' said Arkady. There was pride in his voice, and a shadow of resentment.

'Ladies and gentlemen, welcome!' said Arkady's father. 'Welcome to the Lazarenko Circus! We hope tonight to show you that the world is more strange and wild than you knew: that the human body is the wonder to end all wonders! All we ask is that you watch – and marvel.'

Arkady snorted. 'He says the same thing every night. He doesn't like change.'

The band struck up, and Maiko ran on to the stage to a roar of applause. She back-flipped, loose-limbed and casual, across the floor. Samuel sighed, and the sigh was not for the girl herself but for the ease with which she swept aside the earth's gravitational pull.

Two men ran on: one took her arms and another her feet, and they began to sweep her in wide circles. Another, taller woman spun on to the stage, and began to skip over and under Maiko's falling and rising body.

It was, Vita thought, beauty of a wilder and more vagabond kind than ballet.

Samuel's eyes were as wide as Vita's. Long silks came down from the ceiling, and Maiko swung up and down them as easily as crossing the road, spinning and twisting, and Samuel leaned so far forward he nearly fell out of his seat.

'We've seen the show at least three times a week,' whispered Arkady, jerking his head at Samuel, 'for *years*, and always, *always*, he's like that, when she flies.'

Maiko ran off stage and Samuel sat back up and rubbed his eyes. A single file of poodles marched on stage, followed by Arkady's mother, a tall, stern-faced woman with a large bosom. The dogs leaped in and out of golden hoops, then over one another.

'Are those real gold?' said Vita.

'No, of course not! Just painted cardboard,' said Arkady. 'When I have my own troupe, I won't have hoops – nothing that makes them look foolish. My whole orchestra will be made from birdsong, and people will come from all over the world.'

The dogs were followed by an escape artist, a small Polish man who smiled half a smile while he was dunked in water with his arms padlocked behind him. He was followed by a tightrope walker in a silver leotard. Then Arkady sat up, his back straight.

'Here it is!' he said. 'Watch this!'

A fine-boned man strode on to the stage. Behind him came a line of horses, led by Moscow, her gleaming flank polished with gold dust to make her shine. Vita gasped at the sight of her.

'This is the best part,' said Arkady. 'The liberty act. That's Morgan Kawadza!'

'Kawadza?' Vita turned to Samuel, 'So he's your—'

'My uncle, yes,' said Samuel; and then he was on his feet and walking backwards, into the darkness of the wings, out of sight of the man on stage.

'He's the best in the world,' said Arkady. 'My father nearly cried with happiness when he agreed to join the company. He trained with the Lipizzaners in Vienna.'

'The what?'

'The Lipizzaners! They're the cleverest horses in the world – they were bred to be ridden by Emperors. But watch! You mustn't even blink!'

A waltz began to play. Kawadza clicked his tongue, and called out. The language was not English. 'He taught the horses in English and in Shona – the language in Mashonaland,' whispered Arkady. 'And Moscow speaks Russian, too, of course – I taught her.'

The horses began to dance, moving backwards and side to side to the music.

'Watch Moscow. She's perfect,' said Arkady. 'There's no horse like her. She's a Lipizzan.'

Moscow reared up and walked several steps on her hind legs, whinnying in triumph, then turned a slow pirouette. Kawadza called out to her, telling her she was a queen among horses, that he was proud of her.

'One day soon, Moscow will belong to Samuel,' said Arkady, and he said it in the way that people might say, 'One day, he'll be King.'

The act came to an end, and Kawadza swung himself on to Moscow's back and rode her off stage, to hysterical applause.

Kawadza caught sight of Arkady and stopped. 'Hi, Ark. Where's Sam?' He swung down from Moscow's back. 'Wasn't he just here?'

Arkady was red; the stress of being spoken to by his hero had turned his ears purple. He swallowed. 'Yes, sir. He must have gone to the bathroom, sir.'

'Not still dreaming about that flying, is he?' The man's accent was stronger than Samuel's; it had a rich burr to it, and his vowels stretched out long over his tongue.

116

Arkady swallowed harder. He seemed to be trying to masticate a toad. 'No, sir.'

'Good. I've told him – and I'm telling you, so you can remind him – he doesn't have a choice. Do you hear me?'

'I hear you, sir,' whispered Arkady.

Kawadza glanced out at the audience, rustling in its rich silks and satins. His voice was rough. 'I met a man on the boat coming over – he wanted to be a dancer; he could leap six feet from standing. They looked him over, and they laughed: there could never be a black prince in the ballet. No. The world isn't generous with its imagination to people of my skin: it has already decided what we are. And Samuel is a *child*. It's my job to protect him from disappointment.'

Vita's chest tightened, and she said, 'But—'

He shook his head, quick and hard and sad. 'There can be no but.' Moscow whinnied, and he raised a hand to her flank. 'And anyway, there's no future in tumbling! So he can turn a cartwheel. It's not enough. He'll waste his time on cheap tricks, the world will turn on him and break his heart, and he'll be left with nothing. And without him, who's going to carry on the act when I'm gone? He'll join me with the horses when he's fourteen.' And Morgan Kawadza sighed, looked around once more for Samuel, and strode away, Moscow following.

There was a long pause, in which Vita could think only of Samuel, swinging from the crossbar of the trapeze, his face shining. She made her hands into fists inside her pockets.

Then the band started again, and under cover of the noise Samuel slipped back into his seat.

'Your uncle was just here –' began Vita in a whisper.

'I know. I was behind the fire-eater's buckets.' His whole body was rigid; his shoulders stood up near his ears.

'Are you all right?'

'Fine.' He forced a smile. 'You should watch – it's Lady Lavinia next.'

A beautiful woman, her dark hair falling to her waist, dressed in a sweep of black silk, her fingers covered in scars, came on stage from the other side of the wings. She carried a handful of knives.

118

'You don't want to meet her in a dark alley,' said Samuel. 'Look!'

Lady Lavinia began by juggling four knives. The audience gasped and cheered, and she grinned out at the stage lights and laughed: the laugh of a virtuoso pianist applauded for playing a scale. She added three more knives, then another four, and five more, until there were sixteen knives spinning in the air. She caught them behind her back, spun a knife as long as her arm on her fingertip. She threw apples and knives into the air and then caught them as they fell, the apples neatly halved. The crowd's applause grew deafening.

Vita gripped her chair until the plush cladding peeled away under her fingers. A great spurt of longing rose up in her. *It must feel astonishing, to know how to do that, to make a moving object curve through the air according to your will*, she thought. And it was followed by another thought, one so quiet and new it barely made its way to the surface of her mind. *I could do that.*

Lady Lavinia retreated. 'There's just the elephant still to come,' said Arkady.

'An elephant! That must be amazing.'

Arkady shook his head. 'He's beautiful, yes – so beautiful it hurts – but elephants aren't like the dogs. I wish my father wouldn't have them, but he says you need it for the crowds.'

'Why?'

'The dogs are artistes. They want to work – they want to play. The elephants just want to go home. I've told him and told him, but he won't listen.'

'How do you know the elephant doesn't want to work?'

'I feel it – here,' and he struck his chest. And then he grinned, embarrassed, and turned to watch the stage.

The stage at Carnegie Hall was large – broad enough to hold forty men, shoulder to shoulder. The greatest musicians in the world, Vita knew, had walked across its wooden boards. But it was suddenly dwarfed, rendered small and flimsy and mundane, by the animal that came stepping out of the door on the far side of the stage.

It was bedecked with ribbons; a red silk cloth was

laid over its back, and a gold triangle of silk draped down between its eyes. Somebody had pierced one of its ears with small gold hoops, once at the top and once at the bottom, and a filigree gold chain swung to and fro between the hoops. A silver chain ran between its two front feet. A long thin man, carrying a long thin stick, followed behind, his bald head shining with sweat.

The elephant stood, looking out at the audience, and extended its trunk into the air, as if groping for something. The crowd hushed.

The man shouted an order, and the elephant reared up on its two hind feet, trumpeted, and came crashing down again. The floorboards shook. Splinters spat across the stage; Samuel covered his face with his elbow, and Vita dodged to the left as one flew past her right eye.

Arkady whispered something under his breath that Vita felt confident was not polite.

The man shouted another order, but the elephant did not move. The man shouted again. The elephant stayed where it was, its eyes studying the theatre; the

121

painted ceiling, the rows of watching, hungry faces. Its eyes, which were closer to gold than brown, closed.

Vita felt her own eyes unexpectedly prickling, and the bridge of her nose swelling in the way it did before tears, and she scowled, hard, at her left foot, to banish the water rising in her. The image behind her eyes was not of Carnegie Hall, but of Grandpa, stooped and shackled by something she couldn't see.

The man reached out with the stick; its end caught the light, and Vita saw with a lurch that it wasn't wood at the tip, but knife-sharp iron. It wasn't clear what had happened, but the elephant bellowed, rose to its feet, and reared up to stand on a single hind leg.

The audience whooped and cheered. The man bowed. The elephant was led off stage, back the way it had come, out of the harsh light, and into the dark of the wings.

The house lights rose, and the audience broke into loud chatter. Vita moved to look around the edge of the door into the auditorium, watching the riot of silk skirts flap as the seats emptied. She was just about to ask if she could meet the elephant when her breath halted halfway up her chest.

A man was getting to his feet in one of the boxes, offering his hand to a blonde woman dressed in a dusty-pink gown. He turned, and his eyes met Vita's as she stood, half on and half off the stage.

The man was Victor Sorrotore.

CHAPTER ELEVEN

Fear caught at her body and dragged her backwards, but not before she saw the shock of fury and revulsion that crossed Sorrotore's face. He exited the box at a run.

She darted back into the shadows and turned to Arkady and Samuel. She fought to conquer the fear, to beat it down; she would not let it swallow her.

'We have to go,' she said.

'Go where? This is where we live!' said Arkady.

'Sorrotore's here. He saw me. And, if he finds

me … I have his ring with me.'

Arkady's face creased. 'What ring?'

'I took a ring from his mantelpiece – I think it's evidence of something horrible. Someone came searching for it, under my bed—'

'But—' began Arkady, but Samuel interrupted him. He had seen the panic in her eyes.

'We can't wait here,' he said. 'The audience is allowed to come backstage, if they're rich enough. We'll go out the back way.'

They darted out of the wings, down the corridor. Vita stumbled on the slippery floor and fell, scraping her palms on the wood, but then she was up again and her eyes defied comment. They ran for the stage door, which was ajar, the night air blowing in. Samuel was ahead and darted through it.

Then without warning Samuel jerked back inside, snatched open another door off the corridor and pushed her through it. The three stood in a chaotic props cupboard: masks, capes, and a donkey's head were stacked, teetering, on shelves. A pile of hair showed itself to be a stock of false moustaches.

'What's going on?' hissed Arkady. 'This is hardly the moment to be accessorising.'

'There's a man waiting out there,' said Samuel.

'What did he look like?' asked Vita.

Samuel shook his head. 'I only glimpsed him – but tall, and dark-haired. He had a rich person's face, and a lot of oil in his hair.'

'That sounds like him.' Vita stared around them. The room was windowless. 'Are we trapped?'

'We'll go out the other way,' said Samuel. 'Through the lobby, and the main doors, like everyone else – we'll blend in.'

Arkady grabbed his father's top hat from the shelf. 'Put this on.' It slipped down low over her ears. He snatched up one of the moustaches and tried to fix it to Vita's upper lip.

'Sure,' said Samuel, 'because *that's* the way to blend in – a girl in a moustache and a top hat.'

'Then what?' said Arkady.

Vita put the hat and moustache back on the shelf, and Samuel offered her a dark-brown trilby from a hook. It fitted perfectly. She tilted it low over her eyes.

'Better,' she said. 'Let's go.'

They ran back through the corridors, through two side doors, and they were out, suddenly, in the sparkling lobby, the vast sweeping staircase ahead of them. A family of six – two adults and four children, all exquisitely dressed – were moving slowly down the stairs, the chattering three-year-old setting the pace. Samuel gave Vita a push, and she fell in behind them, trying to look as if she belonged.

At the bottom of the stairs stood the woman in the dusty-pink dress, looking at her watch. Nearby, a girl with a white-blonde plait was winding a thin coat tight around her shoulders.

Look normal, Vita told herself, scanning the crowd. And indeed, to the people passing by, she looked like just another theatregoer, albeit one with unusual taste in hats.

The girl with the blonde plait turned, and Vita's stomach swooped. It was Silk, her mouth turned down like a horseshoe, her eyes focused on something behind Vita.

Vita twisted to follow Silk's glance – to where a

foot now appeared around the corner of the building, and Sorrotore's black cashmere coat swung into view.

Vita slipped behind the tallest of the children as Sorrotore passed by.

It all happened very fast. Silk crossed in front of Sorrotore, her head low, and her hand flickered out.

Sorrotore was of a class trained not to see the poor. He ignored her, and called out to the woman in pink. 'I'm so sorry, my dear – I did say not to wait! I thought I saw an old business associate.' He took her arm, and turned, once, to scan the steps behind him. Vita pressed herself further into the family group, head down, sliding behind the mother's back. Sorrotore gave a hiss of annoyance, turned left, and started walking with the woman in the direction of Central Park. Silk set off in the opposite direction in a walk that was almost a run, and Vita drew a breath.

The family raised six collective eyebrows, finding a girl in a trilby and red boots suddenly in their midst, but the adrenaline thundering through Vita's blood protected her from embarrassment. Arkady and Samuel came running down the steps.

'Did he see you?' said Arkady.

'Are you OK?' said Samuel.

Vita nodded. 'We need to follow.'

Rimsky fluttered down from the rooftop of Carnegie Hall, landing on Arkady's shoulder.

'Follow Sorrotore?' he said. 'Are you mad?'

'No. Follow a girl.'

Samuel smiled his half-smile. 'A specific girl, or just girl pot luck?'

'I'll explain on the way. I know where she'll be.'

CHAPTER TWELVE

It was a cold journey, the walk from Carnegie Hall
to the Bowery; long and cold and dark, but the
stars were out, and New York shone around them.
They went as fast as Vita could go, heads down against
the icy wind, Rimsky riding on Arkady's shoulder. At
least, Vita thought, New York was not easy to get lost
in; most of the streets were laid out in squares, East
22nd leading to East 23rd as neatly as dominoes.

As they walked, Vita explained about Silk, and the
pickpocketing, and the Dakota, and the lock-picking.

'And she said she won't help?' said Samuel.

'Yes. She says she only ever works alone.'

'So …' There was a polite but pointed silence before Samuel said, 'Why are we going to find her?'

Vita took her penknife from her pocket, threw it into the air, and caught it behind her back. Excitement had entered her blood. 'Because! Because she was there, at Carnegie Hall. Waiting. I think she followed Sorrotore. And I want to know why.'

'It could just be a coincidence.'

'I don't think Silk does coincidences.' The Irish girl had a face that said she found the concept of fate insulting.

The streets grew emptier as they went further south, and rougher at the edges; paint peeled, and the restaurants they passed began to advertise more unusual-sounding foods: pig's heart, and sheep's feet. They passed a diner with its menu written on the window in white marker, and above that, the words 'Bowery Bar'.

'This is the Bowery.'

'And we're here because … ?' Arkady's voice tailed away on a question mark.

'Because she said, "You wouldn't last three minutes in the Bowery!" Let's split up,' said Vita. 'She's got to be somewhere round here.' She spoke with infinitely more confidence than she felt.

Arkady set off down the Bowery, Samuel took Prince Street, and Vita headed towards Chrystie Street.

Vita peered down the alleyways as she passed them, seeing only rubbish bins. She passed a musical theatre advertising *Daisy Johnson and Her Bouncing Babies*, dodged a large cat with no tail, skirted a medium-sized rat. Then, just as the cold was seeping into her kneecaps and elbows, and the wind had taken all the blood from her face, she looked down an alley off Hester Street and saw Silk.

But Silk was not alone. She was standing with her back against the wall, and in front of her were the boys Vita had seen outside the Dakota. They looked to be in their early teens, but with the bodies of adults. One boy was long and lanky, the other short, with knots of muscle in his arms and legs.

132

Their voices were full of accusation.

'Liar,' said the taller boy. 'We've got good information you were at the Hall. Give us what you got.'

'I didn't get anything, I said!' said Silk. 'I was just scoping.'

The shorter boy had a face like a lawyer. 'That's not true, though, is it?'

'We don't want trouble,' said the taller boy, 'but we'll make it if we have to. Hand it over!'

'Ah, flip off and leave me alone,' said Silk. Her voice was careless but her face was a vivid white in the street light.

The shorter boy put his hand on Silk's upper arm. She shook him off. 'Don't touch me!'

'Don't think we won't hit you just because you're a girl,' said Tall. 'Those rules weren't made for us.'

Vita glared at the sky and stepped around the corner. 'Let go of her,' she said.

The two boys spun round, their eyes wide, first in surprise, then in half-amused annoyance.

'Who's your friend?'

'What's wrong with her foot?'

'And why's she dressed like a private detective?'

Vita put her hand to her borrowed trilby and flushed. 'I said, let go of her!'

Silk's face was pinched with embarrassment. 'Go away,' she hissed to Vita. 'I'm fine.'

Vita's hand went deep into her pockets, looking for something to throw. She pushed aside the red book, and her penknife – that was precious, that was her own, that was not for moments like this – feeling for something, anything else. There was only the leaflet from Carnegie Hall, rolled into a tight little tube, and some fluff.

The shorter boy turned back to Silk. He took both her fists in one hand, and held them tight. 'Hand over the wallets, and we'll let you go.' And he twisted one of Silk's arms in a sudden jerk, up and round behind her back.

Vita's heart gave a lurch of rage, and without stopping to think she charged at the boy.

He swiped a fist the size of a brick at her. It caught her in the temple, knocking her backwards, filling her eyes with red swirls, but he had to let go of Silk to do so. She darted back down the alley – to a dead end. She let out a gasp, swiftly swallowed.

Vita heard the gasp; and it made her anger roar up and overspill. People do not expect a small girl to be willing to take or inflict pain. So surprise, she knew, was the only thing she had on her side. She hauled herself back up, and kicked out at the short boy's instep with her right foot, holding the wall for balance. She had five seconds, she thought, before the shock of being attacked by a five-foot-nothing with fox-red hair wore off. As he bent forward in pain, she jabbed her knee into his groin.

'Run!' she said to Silk.

Silk did not run. Instead she turned to the tall boy, looked him full in the face, launched forwards, and bit his collarbone. He yelled in surprise, and the two of them closed against each other, kicking and spitting.

The short boy straightened up, dust on his knees, and his hand became a fist with real intentions. Vita ducked sideways and it slammed agonisingly into her shoulder. He grabbed at her arm. She lashed out with her feet, and her free hand reached into her pocket, seized the tightly rolled leaflet, and pushed it as far as it would go up his nostril.

He let out a yell as his eyes filled with water, and Vita bit down at the grasping hand. He struggled free, and stared at her, wild-eyed. 'What's *wrong* with you?'

Footsteps came pounding down the alley now. Vita wiped the hair and sweat from her eyes, locking her thumbs into her fists in readiness. Around the corner came Samuel, followed by Arkady, Rimsky flapping above his head. Arkady's arms were raised, ready to fight, and Samuel's eyes were vivid with anger.

They halted for a second, taking in the scene, then came at a sprint down the alley. Arkady let out a high war cry as they went straight for the two boys.

It was too much for Short. He turned and ran, darting past Arkady, followed by Tall, his mouth open with fear. Rimsky followed, dive-bombing them as they went.

'Are you OK?' asked Arkady.

Vita nodded, unable to catch her breath to speak.

There was a long silence as Silk spat a small amount of blood against the wall, and Vita rearranged her boot.

Silk spoke first. 'You didn't need to do that.'

'Don't worry about it, I—'

'No, I mean – I would have been fine. I didn't need help.'

Various retorts, few of them polite, ran through Vita's imagination. With immense effort, she chose none of them. Instead, she said, 'Will they come after you again?'

'I don't know,' said Silk. 'Probably. If I keep working their patch.' And then, seeing Vita's face crease, she added gruffly, 'Or maybe not. Not worth their time, more likely.'

'You can borrow Rimsky,' said Arkady, 'if you need her. She's like a guard dog.'

Samuel spoke. 'You're bleeding.'

'Who? Me?' said Vita.

'Both of you.'

Vita twisted to see that blood was trickling from her elbow, out through a hole in her coat, torn when she'd fallen. 'Doesn't matter,' she said. She turned to Silk. 'You've got some there, on the side of your head.'

Silk felt, and made a face at the blood on her fingers. 'Ugh.'

Arkady fished out a handkerchief and handed it to Silk. It looked as though cleanliness was a distant memory, but Silk dabbed at her head with it anyway. She looked from Arkady, panting and scowling, to Samuel, brushing off his hands, to Vita, who was watching Silk, her stare unblinking.

Then, very slowly, Silk's mouth began to twitch.

'OK,' said Silk.

'OK what?' said Vita.

'OK, yes. OK, I'll join you. I'll be one of your crew. Just, OK.'

Warmth – enough to beat back the cold of the night – rose in Vita's chest. But she said, 'I thought you never worked with other people.'

Silk shrugged. 'I'll make an exception.' And they each smiled sudden smiles, mirror images of surprise.

'I'll pay you,' said Vita. 'As soon as we sell the emerald – enough to make it worth it, I swear.'

Silk shrugged one shoulder. 'I'd rather not be paid. Not this time.'

A wet drop landed on Vita's face; it was beginning to rain. 'Let's go somewhere we can talk,' she said.

'Can we go somewhere with hamburgers?' asked Arkady. 'I could eat an entire kitchen.'

The diner on the corner was full and bustling, but when Arkady approached, Silk shook her head. 'This place won't let me in. Most places won't, around here.'

'Why not?' asked Arkady.

Silk scowled. 'Why do you think? Here. Down this alley.'

Vita risked a question. 'Why were you there, at Carnegie Hall?'

Silk shook her head again. 'We shouldn't talk here. Wait.' And she led the way at an almost-run, down two more streets, towards a shop door. 'In here, quick, before we get soaked.'

Arkady stopped, his face flushing. 'We can't go in there!' he said.

'Why not?'

'They sell … *brassieres*.'

Vita looked at the window. He was right: the shop-front was a riot of lace and satin, and a mannequin with the eyes of a Major General modelled a corset.

'I thought you said there was food?' said Samuel. 'I'm not eating underpants, not even in the name of friendship.'

'Oh, for goodness' sake! There's a speakeasy in the basement,' Silk said.

'A speakeasy?' said Vita. 'You mean … a bar? But … isn't it illegal?'

'Obviously! Just to remind you, you're looking for somewhere to discuss a crime.'

'Will they even let us in?' asked Arkady. 'Don't you have to be twenty-one?'

'They'll let me in,' said Silk, 'and you're with me.'

Vita looked doubtfully at Silk, and down at the blood on her own elbow and the tear in her coat. But it turned out to be true. Silk marched through the shop, brushing past a row of knickers, and nodded to the supremely respectable-looking old woman behind the counter.

'Evening, Bette,' she said. 'How's business?'

'Evening, Susan.' The woman nodded back, unsmiling. 'Not as good as it could be, not as bad as it might be.' Her accent, like Silk's, had Irish edges to it. She pressed a button under the counter. The wall behind the cash desk clicked, and swung back on a hinge, revealing a flight of rough wooden steps leading downwards. 'Quick, now, before you bring cops poking in among my corsets.'

Silk led the way down the stairs towards a thick black curtain, through which music filtered.

'Who's Susan?' asked Arkady.

'Me, technically,' said Silk. 'But not for years. It's Silk.' She pulled open the curtain, and Vita stepped out on to a gold-lit dance floor.

A four-man band was playing on a tiny stage, and on the marble floor a dozen couples danced. It was not a dance Vita knew – it was something fast and virtuosic, with jerky arms and legs. More couples sat at small circular tables, eating, drinking and, in one case, kissing so enthusiastically they looked, Vita thought, to be welded together. A fire burned under a vast

141

marble mantelpiece, and the room was blissfully warm.

A man behind a counter looked up in surprise as they approached. 'Silk, kid! What are you doing here? You better not be working.'

'I wouldn't work in here,' said Silk. 'You know that. Anyway, I've given up – almost.' Her voice had changed slightly – her vowels were rougher, and harder. 'We're hungry. You got anything?'

'Ah, Silk, not now! I'm in the middle of my shift – and besides, if the cops come and find a bunch of kids round here, I'll be—'

A red flush was spreading up Silk's neck and cheeks. 'You owe me, Tony, since I stole back your grandmother's urn off those kids. You said so yourself.'

Tony sighed. 'How hungry are you?'

'Very!' said Samuel.

'I could eat a horse,' said Arkady.

'Really? You mean that?' The sudden light of the inventor came into Tony's eye. 'I ain't got no horse, but I been experimenting with green turtle hearts and mushroom gravy – you want to try some?'

'Um ...' said Arkady.

'Or can I do you a fishtail fricassee?'

There was a silence so large and so polite it filled the fireplace and went up the chimney.

'Is that a no?' said Tony.

'Do you have anything more ...' Samuel hesitated.

'Normal?' said Arkady.

The man sighed. 'Go in there,' he said, gesturing to a door to the left, 'and don't make a racket. I'll be through in a second.'

The room was empty of people, and much quieter. There was sawdust on the floor instead of shining tiles, and a number of upturned crates, a beer barrel in place of a table, and a smell of paraffin lamps. It was warm. Vita felt her shoulders relax, and drew in a great breath.

'This is where the waiters come for their breaks,' said Silk, sitting on one of the crates. 'But they'll have just started their shifts – they won't be off for hours. We can talk here. Nobody'll hear.'

'Good,' said Vita. 'Tell me – why were you at the circus this evening? It wasn't coincidence, was it?'

143

'No,' said Silk. She reached into her pocket and pulled out a large brown leather wallet, about the size of a paperback book. 'I wanted this.'

'Sorrotore's?' said Vita, though she already knew. The leather had the kind of shine on it that means money.

'Yeah. I followed him to Carnegie Hall from the Dakota and waited outside.'

'You must have been freezing,' said Samuel.

Silk shrugged. 'I wanted it,' she said again. She put the wallet on the upturned beer barrel.

'So you took his wallet,' said Arkady. 'Why?'

'He didn't pay me, that night I worked his party. I stained the uniform they gave me, and he said it was worth more than my night's wages.'

'You broke a statue, too,' Arkady pointed out. 'Vita told us about it. And you stole from his guests.'

'Yeah,' said Silk, and she fixed Arkady with a sharp glare, 'but he doesn't know that. So it was still an injustice. And besides …'

'Besides what?' asked Vita.

'Men like that, they keep a lot in their wallets.

144

And ... then, what you'd said, about what he did. I kept thinking about it. About how men like him always win.'

Vita nodded, and their eyes met, and understanding flickered between them.

'So I thought I'd take a look, and if there was anything worth knowing, maybe I'd find you. Except ... you found me.' And she picked up the wallet and handed it to Vita.

Vita took it gingerly. The leather was soft to the touch; expensive, sleek – like its owner. She felt an unexpected urge to run out to the other room and throw it on the fire.

Instead, she took out the folded dollar bills and handed them to Silk. There were a few receipts, too, and an unopened envelope addressed to 'Mr Victor Sorrotore, The Dakota'.

She was just about to look inside the envelope when the door burst open. Vita barely had time to slip the wallet into her coat and out of sight before Tony barged into the room backwards.

'Here.' He was carrying a tray, which he banged down on top of the beer barrel. 'You kids got no food inquisitiveness, that's your problem. Pedestrian! That's what I call it.' And he stalked out, pulling the door shut behind him.

On the tray were heaped chunks of hot meat, and, next to it, half a loaf of bread, some apples, a couple of California oranges, a slab of butter, and several slices of cheese, each large enough to cover Vita's palm. Standing in the middle of it all was a bottle of ketchup.

'Beefsteak!' said Samuel. 'Excellent.'

There were four jam jars filled with frothing white liquid. Vita sniffed one warily.

'Milk,' she said, relieved. She drank deeply; it was so cold it made the space between her eyes ache. It gave her courage, rising from her stomach outwards.

They ate with their hands, spreading the butter with the bread knife, and using a pencil Samuel found in his pocket to get the ketchup out of the bottle. Vita ate in vast, ravenous bites, swamped by the pleasure of it. They cut the cheese with her penknife and found it rich and salty.

Gradually they slowed, until only Arkady was still going. Samuel, impatient, kicked up into a handstand, one foot leaning against the wall. Arkady reached for his eighth piece of bread.

'Ark, you can't still be hungry?' said Samuel, upside down.

'I believe you should keep eating until it comes out of your ears. Otherwise it's rude to the chef.' He already had a small piece of butter on his chin. At last he finished chewing, and turned to face Vita. Two more expectant pairs of eyes followed suit.

Vita reached into her coat pocket and pulled out the red book. She hesitated for just a moment: looked from one pair of trusting eyes to another, felt her heart roaring in her chest. Then she opened it.

'This is it. This is what we do,' she said.

'You've written it out?' said Silk sharply. She took it up and turned the pages: diagrams, train timetables, to-do lists. 'Is that a good idea? What if someone finds it?'

'I've used initials – no real names. And I keep it on me all the time,' said Vita. 'Nobody can get to it.'

Swiftly she ran through the plan. They'd all three heard it already, but even so they listened with tense and frowning focus.

'Can we have code names, instead of initials?' asked Arkady. 'I'll be Mr Redhanded.'

'No,' said Silk firmly.

'And exactly where's the fountain we have to dig up?' asked Samuel.

'In the walled garden.'

'And where's the walled garden?'

She turned to the next page, where she had copied the blueprint.

'Here.' She pointed. She took Samuel's pencil, and circled it.

'Draw an "X",' said Arkady. 'There's always an "X" on a treasure map.'

Vita scratched a deep 'X' into the blueprint. *'Emerald necklace,'* she wrote.

As she did so, Tony the barman came back into the room, and she pulled the book into her lap. He looked at the almost empty tray, at Arkady's liberally buttered countenance, and nodded.

'Good. I don't like waste.'

But as he bent to pick up the four empty jars, Vita saw his eyes look them up and down – an elevator glance – and saw him frown. He opened his mouth to speak, then grunted, and went out.

Samuel had seen it as well. He turned to Silk. 'He's not going to report us, is he?'

Silk, too, had been watching. 'I don't think so. I didn't like his face, though. I think he thinks we look weird. Strange.'

Vita looked at the boys, and at Silk, and tried to imagine how they would appear to a stranger.

Arkady wore a jersey of such bright red wool you could see him for miles. He had never given back her scarf, which was royal blue, and the two together made him look like a battle flag. Samuel, under his coat, was dressed all in black – sleek, acrobatic clothes, designed not to impede movement. Silk was better, clad in a too-small woollen skirt and a heavy knitted jumper, but her clothes made her look uncared for, ragged – and Vita knew that people fear those who look unsmart, as if they fear poverty itself were contagious. And she, Vita, was most noticeable of all, with her foot arching inwards, in her bright silk boots.

Samuel's thoughts had followed hers.

'What we need,' he said, 'are disguises.'

'Yes!' said Vita. She needed a skirt that would come lower, and hide her left leg.

'Disguises?' said Arkady. 'Why?'

'What you wear changes the way people treat you,' said Samuel. 'You know – some clothes say, *Love me*, and some say, *Believe me*, and some say, *Oh just ignore me*.'

'We need the kind of clothes that say, *We've never had a dangerous or illegal thought in our lives*,' said Vita. 'If anyone sees us on the journey to the house, we need people to approve of us and then just completely forget us.'

'What sort of clothes are those?' asked Silk. She looked down at her bare knees defensively.

A picture came to Vita of the kind of clothes the Royal children had worn at home.

'Expensive, I think,' said Vita. 'Nobody suspects

the rich. Clothes that say, *My surname is the same as the name of a bank, and it's not a coincidence.* That kind of look.'

'Grey,' said Silk firmly. 'Grey or brown – those look respectable. Mud colours. Grey trousers and jackets for the boys, dresses for us.'

'Right,' said Samuel, 'How are we going to do that?'

'Mug a priest?' suggested Arkady.

Vita glared. All eyes turned to Silk.

She flushed. 'I'm a pick*pocket*, not a pick-entire-bloody-outfit,' she said.

'Couldn't you steal enough cash for us to buy new clothes?' said Arkady.

'No.' Silk's face was hard and blank. 'Or … yes, I could. But I don't want to.'

'But—' began Arkady.

'I'm sick of it, all right?' Silk's shoulders rose high, and she spat her words. 'I don't want to trick and twist and lie and run! You don't know what it's like, all the time, to have your heart in your throat like a stuck chicken bone. I want to be like you three. I want to be a normal kid.'

151

'I wouldn't say any of us is *normal*,' said Arkady. He sounded insulted.

'I mean that someone feeds you, don't they? Someone cares about you. Someone makes you sandwiches and washes your clothes and does up your buttons if you can't reach them. Nobody does that for me.'

For all her toughness, her sharp elbows and sharp chin, she suddenly looked as breakable as bone china. She glared down at her grubby nails. 'So, no. I won't do it.'

A silence fell. Vita, feeling all thumbs and knees, tried to think of something comforting. She leaned over to where Silk sat, and touched her ankle, briefly, with her fingertips. The world felt unjust, misshapen.

But Samuel's face had brightened – had suddenly turned electric and vivid. 'I know!' he said.

'What?' said Arkady.

'Tell us?' said Vita. His hope was infectious.

'The Lost and Found! Practically every place in this city has a Lost and Found – every movie theatre, every train station, every restaurant. Even the place where they sell tickets for the Statue of Liberty has one!'

Silk raised her fine blonde eyebrows. 'People don't forget their *trousers*.'

'They do in hotels!' he said. 'In all those drawers! All we have to do is scrub ourselves, so we look clean, go to every hotel, and tell them a friend of ours left behind a pair of trousers – or a jacket or a dress or whatever – in the room, and ask if they've got any in the Lost and Found.'

'It's a brilliant idea!' said Vita.

'When?' said Silk.

'Tomorrow!' said Vita. 'As soon as we can.'

'And then?' said Arkady.

'Then we'll be ready to go!'

'Right,' said Silk. She turned and looked at Vita; at her thin hands, at her bloodied elbow. 'So if he's climbing the wall, and *he's* taming the dogs, and I'm picking the lock to the walled garden – what are *you* doing?'

Samuel and Arkady turned to Vita, as if the question had not occurred to them.

'Well … it's my family's emerald,' she said, reasonably enough.

'But what can you *do*?' asked Silk.

Vita's brain drew a total blank. She thrust her hands in her pockets, and her fingers met her penknife. She thought of Lady Lavinia, and her sharp-eyed watchfulness.

'Wait a second.' The mostly devoured loaf of bread still lay on the beer barrel next to the bread knife. She took it, an apple, and an orange, and set them side by side on the mantelpiece.

'My grandpa taught me to do this,' she said.

She crossed to the far end of the room, took the bread knife, the steak knife, and her own penknife in one hand, and without pausing to make sure the others were watching her, threw the knives over their heads at the mantelpiece. They yelped and ducked, and twisted to stare.

The bread knife had sliced a chunk off the apple. The steak knife had stuck in the bread. And her own Swiss Army knife had cut straight to the centre of the orange, filling the room with the scent of the faraway

154

sun. In fact, she had been aiming to slice the apple exactly in two, like Lady Lavinia in Carnegie Hall, but she did not admit it.

'I can do that,' she said. 'I'm the *just-in-case*.'

They left quietly, moving in single file. The room had filled up since they arrived, and several men sat on stools at the bar, all varying degrees of drunk.

'Hey! Kid … Wha's yer name? Jack Welles's grandkid!'

Vita whipped around. Sitting on one of the stools was Dillinger, even grubbier now than in the Park, his shirt untucked, a saliva-wet cigar hanging from his mouth.

Samuel stepped forwards, and Silk's hand was forming a fist, but Vita shook her head.

'Let me,' she said. Up close, his skin was grey. His fingers were gripping the edge of the bar, as if the room were in motion.

'It's the girl who plays with fire,' Dillinger slurred. Spittle flew from his mouth on the *s* of 'plays', and she recoiled. 'Aren't you out kind of late, for a kid and a cripple?'

Vita flinched backwards, then collected her breath, and stepped forwards. 'What do you want?'

'What do I want?' And he laughed. 'I don't want anything. But you want something. You want your granddaddy's house back. Don't you?'

Vita did not move.

'Well, you ain't going to get it, kid. And pretty soon you won't want it back, not when he's through with it.'

'What are you talking about?'

But he was laughing again, amused at some thought that had bubbled up from the grimy recesses of himself. 'You'll find out. He was searching for that necklace you told him about. You was real helpful – you know that? – filling him in.'

Vita only stood and waited.

'But now he's gotten tired of treasure-hunting. And he's worried about the questions being asked. And when he gets worried he gets mean. Business ain't going as easy as it was. So he's set a date.' Dillinger belched, and winced. 'Next week.'

'A date for *what*?'

Dillinger peered at her. 'He's got something against

you. It's not just that you took that ring, though he'll get you for that, for sure. But I never seen him like this. I never seen him hate a kid before. You really got under his skin, you know that?'

'Next week *what*?' asked Vita again.

But he turned to the barman. 'A scotch on the rocks,' he said, 'and don't be shy with it.' He thumped the bar and his eyes, unmoored by drink, rolled briefly backwards leaving only the whites showing.

Vita turned away, but he called after her.

'Did you hear what I said, kid? It's fire you're playing with. Don't get burned!'

CHAPTER THIRTEEN

Vita's mother was waiting up when she got home, and she was white with fear and anger. Vita had known she would be. The ensuing conversation was bad – somewhere, Vita thought later, when her tears had dried, between thunderstorm and miniature apocalypse.

'I can't be here to watch you, not like at home!' said her mother, and there were tears in her eyes, too. 'And you know you're not strong!'

'I am!'

Her mother bit her lips together; her face was still wild with residual fear. 'You're a *child*! I told you I was trusting you and Grandpa not to get into trouble – please, Vita, don't make me regret it! I couldn't bear it!'

At last the storm abated.

'Promise me you won't do it again?' asked her mother, once she had bathed Vita's cut, and Vita said, 'I promise,' and kissed her mother and ran to her bed before she could be asked to define exactly what it was she was promising.

Vita was in bed and half asleep, with the red book under her pillow, before she remembered Sorrotore's wallet. She sat bolt upright and listened to the apartment. All was quiet; the only sound was the thrum of the city outside.

She crept down the hall and grabbed her overcoat from its hook. The wallet, when she fished it out, had that faint scent to it: leather, and some kind of perfume; and power.

She pulled out an envelope, folded in half, and a few receipts.

The receipts told her nothing except that Sorrotore had expensive tastes – one was for twelve bottles of Perrier-Jouët 1904 champagne – so she tore open the envelope.

A single sheet of headed writing paper was wrapped around scraps of newsprint.

All of them were news reports about fires: buildings destroyed, across the city.

The covering letter read:

Victor,

Progress on various projects; see enclosed. Keep me updated on your latest. Don't waste time. Fair Homes is waiting to move in and make the Hudson Castle Hotel a reality.

Yours, in haste,

Westerwicke

She spread out the enclosed press cuttings. They seemed to have no connection to Sorrotore, or to one another. They were all old buildings, and old buildings catch fire easily. Except, she saw, as she read on, that one company seemed to be building on the burned-out spaces, post-fire: Fair Homes Enterprises.

Fair Homes, according to the newsprint, claimed to produce 'affordable housing for hardworking New Yorkers'. But Vita frowned as the article went on: it seemed the buildings it constructed were all luxury apartments, with doormen and gold-plated swimming pools; the kind of buildings that suggested it was your duty to refrain from being poor.

She read closer. The articles mourned the loss of buildings that had been protected: churches and theatres, places that should have shaped the history of the city. Buildings that took up valuable space in the heart of the most desirable areas.

She stared down at the list. A block of apartments on East 23rd Street had caught fire overnight; one person had been injured, and an elderly man had died later of smoke inhalation. The street name was familiar; had she walked down it? She read on: The Old Hotel, Columbus Avenue, had burned beyond repair.

The name prickled with familiarity. She took

her penknife in her fist, flicking at the tweezers with her thumb, thinking, digging backwards in her memory – and then it came to her.

The papers on Sorrotore's desk.

The Old Hotel had been sold for $200. And now it was gone.

She looked back at the press cuttings, and, slowly, she began to piece it together. Sorrotore bought old buildings, under the names of different companies; he burned them; then Westerwicke built on them.

How many buildings had he promised to save, the way he had promised to save Grandpa's? How much money, she wondered, were he and Westerwicke making?

Her arms and hands were cold, but her heart was hot. She thought of Dillinger's glee at his own words: *'It's fire you're playing with ...'*

A drunk with a pun. And what else had he said? *'He's set a date. Next week.'*

That was it, then, she thought. That was why Sorrotore wanted Hudson Castle; to burn it to the ground. And she had almost no time at all. *'Next week'*: that could mean any time from Monday, or even Sunday. Today was Wednesday.

She fell asleep with the red book clutched to her chest. Sorrotore went stalking through her dreams, his face bearing ever closer; a cold and unlovely bedfellow.

CHAPTER FOURTEEN

The next day the raid on the Lost and Found boxes of New York City began.

'We need to move fast,' said Vita. She told them, as briefly as she could, about the papers; about the fresh jolt of urgency running through their plan.

'But what is he actually doing?' said Arkady.

'I think he cons people – threatens them, cheats them, I don't know – into selling old buildings – beautiful ones, in beautiful places – very cheap. Places it would be illegal to knock down, because they're protected. And then gives orders for them to be burned down, so he can build something new.'

'So *did* your grandpa sell his house?' said Silk.

'No, no, no! But it's the same thing: Sorrotore's going to set it on fire. And there's no time.' The panic rose in her, and she forced it back down, away from her heart. 'Let's split up. We'll meet back here tonight.'

They walked and ran, between them, almost the length and breadth of New York. Silk, who knew the city best, split it into sections on Vita's map. She did not glance at Vita's foot, but gave her the places nearest to Carnegie Hall.

Silk uncovered one small adult's grey jacket in Chumley's speakeasy in Greenwich Village, which almost fitted Arkady, and Vita found an ankle-length blue velvet dress at the terrifyingly marble-and-gold Waldorf Hotel. The dress was hideous and too tight, but it radiated sweetness and nursery rhymes. It also came down to the floor, hiding her left calf and ankle. Samuel found an entire suit of boy's clothes, in a thick brown material, recovered from the Algonquin Hotel.

He looked victorious, and angry. 'They wouldn't give it to me at first, so I told them I was a houseboy for the family. Then they handed it over without blinking.'

Arkady looked at his friend: at his fury, and the hurt in his eyes. '*Chyort*,' he said. 'I hope you spat on them.'

Samuel tried to smile. 'That wouldn't have helped much,' he said.

Finally, just as Silk was beginning to despair, it occurred to her to ask at the Lyceum Theatre if anyone had left behind a coat in the cloakroom in the last month. She was rewarded with a white hooded cloak trimmed with swan feathers, which reached almost to the ground. It was a little greying at the sleeve and neck, and the swan feathers were possibly a bit much, but it was undeniably smart.

'Let's meet somewhere posh!' Vita had said. 'As a test! If people don't stare, we'll know we look right.'

'The Plaza Hotel. It's just on the edge of Central Park – it's the smartest place in New York,' Silk said. She was using Vita's penknife to trim back the swan feathers from her cuffs. 'The old women who go there for tea can guess how rich you are by the way you sneeze. If nobody stares at us there, nobody ever will.'

Samuel hesitated. Then: 'People will still stare,' he said.

'What do you mean?' said Vita.

'People will still stare. At me. If we try to go somewhere rich. Even if I'm dressed up, they'll still stare.'

Vita felt herself colour, a flood of red rising up her cheeks. 'I'm so sorry,' she said quietly. 'I should have thought of that. Let's—'

'No,' said Samuel. He fingered the brown cloth of the suit jacket. There was doubt in his face, but something else, too: the same determination that had once allowed a four-year-old boy to do secret backflips across a pitch-black bedroom. His jaw worked as he set his teeth. 'We'll go anyway. I want to. If they stare at me, I'll stare back.'

The Plaza Hotel was the kind of place you expect to find people clad in velvet and swan's feathers, who pitch their voices low and their eyebrows high. It was for people who did not walk but *swept*.

Vita did her best to sweep as she made her way up to the vast door. She nodded to the doorman and went in, keeping her chin as high as it would go.

A man followed behind her. His eyes, had she turned to see them, were unsure: they studied not her face but her feet, covered by the floor-length dress. His hand was tattooed with a spitting cat.

'Over here!' called Arkady. The three stood inside the Palm Court, by the central bar, on which stood a vast golden statue of the Greek god Hermes. Across the ceiling, hanging from sturdy ropes, were autumnal wreaths and bowers, so that the room appeared to be half dining room, half exquisite forest. Vita stared. Money shone from the faces of every person there.

A family group, dining on pressed chicken and savoury jellies, glanced over at Samuel, then looked away. Samuel lifted his chin and glared back. It was, Vita thought, the kind of glare that could boil ice.

'Trees and leaves indoors,' said Arkady. He wrinkled his nose at the potted palm trees that filled the room. 'But no birds. Ridiculous.' Then he held out his jacket to Vita. 'What do you think?'

Vita looked them up and down. Both boys wore ties; all four of them were scrubbed clean. 'If we looked any more innocent,' she said, 'we'd be arrested for it.' She felt the excitement rise in her. 'We're ready. We go tomorrow! It's going to happen!' And she spun around, so her dress flared out around her shins, showing her bright red boots.

Across the room, the man with the cat tattoo nodded to himself, and quietly stepped outside.

'Guys,' said Samuel. He spoke without moving his lips. 'I think we should go.'

'Why?' said Silk. 'Are people staring? Show me, and I'll—'

'No. I think someone's recognised us.'

'Us?'

'Recognised Vita. Let's go.'

But as they moved for the vast glass doors out to the street, the man came back in, with two others following behind, both clad in grey suits. Their eyes were fixed on Vita. She felt her body seize up.

Samuel looked from Vita's face, to the men, and back.

'Run!' he whispered. 'I've got an idea. Ark, I need your help.'

'But—' began Silk.

'Just run!' Samuel had that same sharp, unswerving look that Vita had seen on his face as he jumped out of the midnight window. 'Go!' he said. He pushed past the other three, rubbing the inside of his elbow, rolling his shoulders, as if about to mount the trapeze and fly. Arkady ran after him.

'Come on,' hissed Silk. 'I know a way out.' And she darted to the left, towards the kitchen entrance. Vita ran, trying to keep her weight on her right foot, but three men were coming after them, moving as unobtrusively as they could through the tables.

Arkady turned to Samuel. They had three seconds in which to whisper, their eyes on the men.

'*Listo*, Sam?'

'Ready,' said Samuel.

'*Hep!*' said Arkady, and held out his two hands, fingers intertwined. Samuel bit his lips together, set his foot in the stirrup of Arkady's hands, and leaped like a ballet dancer into the air.

He landed sitting astride the shoulders of the statue of Hermes, scrambled up into a crouch, leaped again, and seized hold of one of the ropes that bore the autumnal wreaths. Leaves showered down across the room. A woman in a pearl-dotted beret choked on her tea. A small child cheered. A fluffy white poodle barked.

Samuel swung on the rope, casting his weight back and forth, then let go and flew across the room. He pointed his feet, stretched out both arms, and landed in the uppermost leaves of one of the palm trees, which fell with a crash. It overturned two tables and a visiting Russian Ambassador, striking one of the grey-suited men on the shoulder.

Several waiters yelled and swore, and staff came running out of the kitchen to find out the cause of the chaos. People were crowding round, but Samuel was up, disentangling himself from palms, dodging hands, running towards the kitchens.

The tattooed man pushed aside a shouting waiter and reached out his hand to grab at Samuel's back. Arkady whistled, and the miniature poodle barked.

He pointed, and the man found a small ball of toothy fluff flying at his upper thigh.

The two boys sprinted to the kitchen, dodging past staff coming in the other direction, then hurled themselves out of the back door into an alley.

Silk and Vita had just reached the end of the alley. Now they turned and waited for the boys.

'I guess –' Samuel gasped for breath, and his eyes were alight – 'we gave them a reason to stare.'

Across the road stretched the black expanse of Central Park.

'That way!' said Vita.

'Can we have a pact, next time,' said Samuel as they ran, 'that when one of us says run, you have to run?'

It had begun to rain, and the ground was slippery. They were halfway across the road when the door of the kitchen swung open again, and the men came out.

'Hey! Slow down! We ain't gonna hurt you!' called one.

Silk swerved, and Vita tripped over her own foot in the middle of the road and cursed. Cars rushed by, inches from her. She hauled herself up and darted over the road, weaving in and out of traffic. The others were waiting, and they threw themselves into the darkness of Central Park.

It was very different from the autumn-bright place she and Grandpa had walked through. He would be furious if he saw her now – he would think she had broken her promise – but Vita shoved the thought away. It was pitch black and she led the way at a run, down the empty tree-lined avenue, past the spot where Dillinger had grabbed her arm. The footsteps behind them were closing in – Vita dodged behind a dripping wet bush and the others followed, panting.

Footsteps neared them, then passed them, heading further into the Park.

'Come out, kid! This isn't a game.'

Vita crouched, utterly still, rain dripping off her face. She was aware it was not a game.

The voice came again; it was impossible to tell from exactly where. 'Just give us that ring, and everyone gets to go home.'

The four faced one another amid the leaves.

'What are we going to do?' breathed Silk. There was a crackle of panic in her voice. 'We can't outrun them.'

'Yes you can,' whispered Vita, for the men were unfit, built for muscle not speed. 'Only I can't. You should go! They're only interested in me.'

Arkady snorted. 'Don't be ridiculous.'

Vita cast a desperate look into the Park. The path forked ahead, leading to one wide footpath and one narrow one. The autumn leaves had fallen so thickly they almost hid the manhole cover in the middle of the narrow path.

The same manhole cover down which Dillinger had disappeared.

'If you come out now,' came a voice through the dark, beyond the trees, 'we'll be in a much better mood than if you come out later.'

'Someone should scalp the little brat.'

The footsteps began to return towards them.

Vita looked again at the manhole cover. Then she crept, her left foot dragging through the wet puddles, water soaking into the red silk of her boot, and bent to grab the metal edge of it. She heaved. It lifted a quarter of an inch.

'In here!' she hissed.

Arkady stared at her. 'Vita!' he whispered. 'That's the *sewer*!'

'It's not!' She struggled with the disc of metal. It weighed as much as a grown man. 'It's OK. Come *on*!' she said to the manhole cover, and heaved again.

'How do you know?'

'I saw someone else do it. That man, Dillinger.' Their faces were loose with astonishment. 'Here, help me, one of you! – I can't lift it.'

All three scrambled to her side and together they lifted the cover clear.

'Quick!' said Vita, looking back over her shoulder. They were out in the open, vulnerable.

Silk looked down, disgusted, at the cold blackness beneath their feet, but the burr of voices was coming closer. She set her foot on the ladder and disappeared into the dark. Arkady followed at a swift scrabble. Samuel gave Vita a push.

'Go.'

Vita went as fast as she could, which was not fast, her left foot twisting and slipping against the metal rungs of the ladder set into the brick wall. An agonising pain shot up towards her knee.

She was only halfway down when above her Samuel gasped, and the cover clanged shut, encasing them all in darkness. He did not follow her down the ladder, but leaped outwards, dropping past her into the black and landing in a practised crouch on the floor. Then he came shinning back up the ladder beneath her.

'Do you need a hand?' he asked, his voice low.

'I'm OK,' she said, but his presence on the rung below – the knowledge that if she slipped she would be caught – helped, and she moved more swiftly, gritting her teeth.

They stood, the four of them, at the foot of the ladder. Vita could not see the walls; could not see her own hand in front of her.

'Does anyone have a torch?' asked Silk.

Samuel felt in his pockets. 'I've got matches,' he said.

He lit one, and in its flickering light they could see

they were standing at the opening of a tunnel – to the left, there was a black, wet wall.

'Shh,' said Silk. 'Listen!'

There was only the drip of water; and then voices came from above them.

'This is ridiculous. Let's get out of here.'

There was a snort: cruel, and frightened. 'I'm not going back to him without that ring: you can if you want. They can't have gone far – she's a cripple!'

Vita's eyes widened, and, voicelessly, she pointed down the dark tunnel. If the men thought to lift the manhole cover, they must see only darkness.

'How do we get out?' whispered Arkady as they walked.

'There are hundreds of manholes all over New York,' said Vita.

Samuel nodded in the match-light. 'We'll keep going until we see a ladder.'

'Some of them will be bolted down,' said Silk.

'But not all. We'll just go on until we find one that isn't.'

Samuel led the way, holding his matches up high until they burned down to the very tips of his fingers.

'I've only got five matches left,' said Samuel after a few minutes. 'I should probably save them.'

So they went on, Samuel and Vita with their hands on the left wall, Silk and Arkady on the right, feeling for a ladder to the sky above.

Absolute darkness does strange things to time. Every step Vita took was the same as the previous one; it became like a dream, a nightmare, edging in silence through the dark. Had she not heard Arkady's breath beside her, the sound of Silk's feet, the brushing of Samuel's coat sleeve against the wall, she would have doubted she was moving forward at all. The only other sounds were the dripping of water, and an echoing scratching sound from the tunnel ahead of them. Vita clenched her fists and prayed it was not a rat; and then, on second thought, prayed that it was.

They walked on, and the tunnel grew tighter, close enough to touch both walls at once. It may have been only minutes, or far longer, when Samuel, turning a bend in the underground space, stopped suddenly, and Vita walked into his back.

'Why have you stopped?' she spoke in a whisper; the dark impelled silence.

'There's something up ahead.'

'What?' said Arkady.

'Light.'

'Thank God,' breathed Silk – but Vita's already cold hands grew colder.

'It's can't be sunlight,' she said. 'It's dark outside, remember?'

She could not see the faces of the others, but she could hear Arkady's groan. Trying not to shake, she stepped around the corner, keeping her left side pressed against the wall.

The passage continued for thirty paces, then twisted again, and from beyond the bend in the tunnel came a yellow glow.

'What now?' asked Arkady.

'We could go back,' said Vita. 'And hope they've gone.'

'This isn't supposed to happen!' said Silk. Her voice had tears in it, but she swallowed them. 'I would never have come down here if I was working by myself! This is why you can't trust people! You end up buried underground.'

'Shh,' said Arkady. 'They'll hear you!'

'I don't care!' But she lowered her voice.

'I say we go on,' said Vita. And although her whole body felt heavy enough to crack through the floor, she led the way.

She went as silently as possible, lifting her left foot with agonising care, laying it down without a sound. Samuel, with the feather-light toe-heel walk of an acrobat, followed, and after him an animal tamer and a pickpocket: people accustomed to silence. So it was that the men did not hear their coming.

Vita looked around the corner, and choked back her gasp of fear. The tunnel was wider, enough to allow six men to pass abreast. Hurricane lamps stood on the floor, and electric torches had been hung, swinging, from the ceiling.

A row of tables stood pushed against one wall, and ten men stood over them, pouring clear liquid into glass bottles. Others pasted labels on the bottles:

Muscovite Vodka. More men, dressed in dark colours, stacked the bottles into crates. Some smoked while they worked, cigarettes hanging limply from their mouths. The air was dank, and cold.

But that was not what made Vita gasp. A briefcase had been slung on to a large wooden box in the corner, and next to it lay two rifles and a handgun, wet with the grit of the tunnel floor. And, leaning over the briefcase, counting stacks of bills into it, was Dillinger.

Vita stared at the guns; at their cold, matter-of-fact presence, large as the room itself. Dillinger closed the case, straightened up, and lurched backwards to lean against the wall, his face contorting, the crown of his sandy hair pressed against the dripping wall.

'He's still drunk,' breathed Silk behind her.

Vita ducked back round the corner.

'We're trapped,' she whispered.

Samuel shook his head. 'There's a ladder out,' he said. 'Did you see?'

Vita had seen; beyond the busy workspace, where the tunnel narrowed again, lit by torchlight, there was a ladder leading upwards.

'We could just wait,' said Samuel. 'They have to leave sometime.' But as he spoke, his voice caught, and he jerked backwards a few steps.

'Someone's coming down it,' he breathed.

Vita put one eye around the corner, trusting the dark to envelop them. A shining pair of leather shoes appeared on the ladder, followed by a calf-length black cashmere coat.

Sorrotore landed with a thump on the floor of the tunnel. Vita's heart twisted in her chest as he glanced around at the men loading bottles. They did not meet his eye, but the speed of their work suddenly increased.

'Dillinger!' said Sorrotore. 'What's the hold-up? You were due up four minutes ago. The lorries can't wait. We can't have any more mistakes!' His eyes were wilder than they had been at the party; there was stress written in the pasty colour of his skin.

Dillinger still leaned against the tunnel wall. Now he opened his eyes, his mouth turned down so the edges almost reached his neck.

'I couldn't make them work faster.' His words came

out thick and slow. 'Why don't you threaten to kill them? That usually works.'

And he closed his eyes again.

Sorrotore strode up to him. Vita thought he was going to attack him, but he only picked up the suitcase. He called out a name – 'Kelly!' – and a man, large as a doorway, came to his side.

'What the hell's going on with Dillinger?' said Sorrotore.

'He's drunk,' said Kelly.

'I can see that, thank you. Why? Since when?'

Kelly shrugged. 'He was talking about that Hudson Castle – said he didn't like being set on a kid, and especially not a cripple.'

'He's been whining to the men?' Sorrotore's voice was ugly.

Kelly looked alarmed at the effect his words had had. 'I didn't say that! I just meant, he's been drinking hard for months now, and it's gotten worse in the last few days. He hasn't been sober for maybe … seventy-two hours.'

'He can be drunk on his own time, but not on

mine. I spent fifteen years building all this up from nothing! I didn't do it by employing losers. He screwed up the Louie Zwerback job, too. I've got people sniffing round. Get rid of him.'

Kelly hesitated, his face lurid and uncertain.

'What do you mean?'

Sorrotore shrugged. 'You know exactly what I mean.' He turned to the rest of the men. 'All right,' he called. 'Move this stuff out. You've got two minutes.'

The small space became chaotic and unbearably loud as the rattle of bottle racks being stacked quickened, and the men began to ferry the boxes up the ladder to the street.

The four children waited, crouched in the darkness around the corner, barely daring to breathe.

In an astonishingly short time, the room was clear; only the tables remained, a few puddles of spilt vodka, and the large wooden box under a single light.

Sorrotore strode to the wooden box and lifted the lid. He reached inside, fished out a small tortoise, and dropped it on the floor. Then, with some grunting and scrabbling, he lifted out the larger one.

'Kelly.' Sorrotore clicked his fingers, and the man came. 'I'm running low on cash – just a temporary thing.' But Kelly's eyes showed, just for a second, his scepticism before he masked it. 'So I need the jewels off the tortoises. Chuck the bodies down the tunnel somewhere when you're done.'

'And what about Dillinger?'

Dillinger was still slumped against the wall; Sorrotore turned to him while Kelly hovered uneasily, his vast arms uncertain by his sides. Sorrotore picked up the smallest of the guns and cocked it.

Vita could not help it; she retched – a small, desperate sound that rang through the silent air.

Sorrotore's eyes narrowed. He took three steps towards the bend in the tunnel, his nostrils flaring, sniffing. Beside her, Arkady stiffened, and got ready to spring.

A voice called from the open space above the ladder. 'Trucks are leaving now, boss.'

Sorrotore grunted, sighed, and strode back to the ladder. Kelly made to follow him, and Sorrotore turned to him with a look of disgust.

'Where do you think you're going? I said, do the tortoises – and take care of Dillinger.'

'What, now?' said Kelly.

'Now,' said Sorrotore, and disappeared up the ladder. The clang of the manhole cover closing rang through the tunnel.

Kelly crossed to Dillinger, his face miserable. On the first punch, Dillinger crumpled to the ground. On the third, he ceased to moan. Kelly sighed. He lifted the gun, and checked that it was loaded.

Vita, a planner to her very bones, acted without a plan. She reached into her coat pocket and clenched her penknife. She left it closed, and threw it through the dark. But fear made her stiff and off-balance, and instead of hitting Kelly on the temple, it struck him on the side of the nose. He staggered and dropped to his knees, a child's wail coming from his mouth. He turned in their direction.

Samuel stepped forward, but Silk had already gone. She made a noise somewhere between a moan and a roar and came out of the darkness like a bullet. Her mouth remained open in a noiseless gape as she

186

dodged round Kelly's kneeling form, snatched up the gun from where it lay, hesitated for a split second, and then swung it at the back of Kelly's head. The man slumped, face forwards, on the ground.

Silk looked down, chest heaving, eyes wide, at what she had done. 'Is selfastonishment a word?' she asked. 'Because if not, I need it to be now.'

Five minutes later, Dillinger opened an eye and saw four faces clustered over his.

'What's goin' on?' He muttered. 'Who are you? Get lost.' And then, looking up at Samuel, he spoke a single, unrepeatable word. Arkady's head whipped backwards and Silk swore. Vita let out a hiss, and her eyes sought Samuel's. Only Samuel remained motionless, staring, hot with anger. Dillinger groaned, and his eyes closed again.

'Let's go,' said Arkady, and he ran to pick up the largest tortoise, which had retreated entirely into its shell.

Vita picked up the smaller tortoise; its head waved frantically, staring around the dark space.

'What about him?' she said, jerking her head at Dillinger.

'Leave him,' said Silk.

'No!' said Samuel. 'That makes us as bad as them.'

'It doesn't!' Silk's voice was shrill, still jittery with adrenaline.

'You heard what he said, Sam,' said Arkady. His face was tight with fury. 'We don't have to help him.'

'If we leave him, they'll kill him when they come back,' said Samuel.

'Why do *you* care? He'd kill us!' said Silk.

Sweat beaded on Vita's upper lip. 'I agree with Samuel,' she said. 'We have to take him with us.'

'That's easy for you to say!' said Silk. Her hands were shaking. 'It won't be you carrying him up the bloody ladder.'

Vita jerked as if stung. The space behind her eyes smarted, and she fought the feeling back. It would be terrible to cry.

Silk winced. 'I didn't mean it like that …'

'Fine. I know,' said Vita, and turned away, so Silk would not see her face.

'Ark and I will carry him,' said Samuel. 'Ark, come on.'

Arkady sighed, and moved to his friend's side. The two boys bent down; for a second they strained in the darkness, then they straightened, the man hanging between them.

'How do we get him up the ladder?' said Arkady.

Vita went first. Her balance was not good, and it took all her focus to get herself up to the street. She crouched by the mouth of the hole, keeping watch.

The other three children took Dillinger between them. Samuel led, climbing with one hand, his other arm clamped under Dillinger's armpit. Arkady and Silk pushed his knees and feet. At one point they nearly dropped him, and Dillinger's forehead scraped against the wall.

They darted back down for the tortoises, the boys carrying the largest between them, Silk holding the smaller one under her arm. On the top rung she handed it to Vita, and scrambled up into the street. Its rubies, spelling out her name, glinted in the street lights.

They half dragged, half carried Dillinger down two blocks, then dumped him in an alley.

'If this was a storybook,' said Arkady, 'when he woke up, he would have to do us a good deed.'

'He won't,' said Samuel, and he spoke with absolute certainty.

Dillinger was beginning to stir. Samuel bent and pulled the man's elegant silver watch from his wrist. He stamped on it, shattering the glass face, and turned away.

'Wait a second,' said Vita. She brought her aching left foot down on the face of the watch, grinding as hard as she could with the heel. Silk spat on the silver links. Arkady stamped last and hardest, his eyes on his friend.

Samuel kicked the watch into the grate of the open drain. He looked a little less exhausted. 'Let's go,' he said.

They were halfway back to Carnegie Hall when they became aware of someone following them. Arkady and Samuel carried the large IMPERIUM tortoise; Vita carried VITA. Silk was up ahead, choosing the quietest streets, staying in the shadows, when the footsteps came.

They were not the light-footed, slyly slow footsteps of the men in grey. These were official footsteps, heavy with the confident authority of the law.

'Just keep walking,' murmured Vita.

'Hey! Kids! Hey! What's that you got there?' A figure in dark blue, a wooden truncheon in one hand, stood at the far end of the long street. 'We're looking for a couple kids who busted up the Plaza – you wouldn't know anything, would you?'

They did not turn round. They passed under a street lamp, the light glinting off the IMPERIUM diamonds. At the sight of the gems the policeman broke into a run.

'Stop! Hey, you!'

Samuel twisted to stare, his eyes wide.

'Run! The pact! Run!' said Silk, and all four began to sprint, Arkady and Samuel vanishing around the corner clutching the tortoise between them.

Vita's hair flew wild in the air, and the street was a blur. Silk was ahead of her, far ahead now, her plait thumping against her back; Vita could hear the policeman's footsteps, closer and closer, and though she tried to fire her legs forwards she wasn't going fast enough.

The policeman was barely ten feet away when Silk turned suddenly and came sprinting back. She wrenched the tortoise from Vita's hands. '*Go!*' said Silk. '*Get out of here!*'

Vita tried to tug it back, but Silk gave her a great shove, and Vita stumbled. Knowing she was beaten, she darted round the corner and out of sight. Samuel and Arkady were there, crouched behind two dust-bins, waiting, their faces tight with fear.

The policeman's voice called out, and Silk's answered. There was a brief commotion, but the wind roared again, and Vita couldn't hear above her thumping heart. She risked peering round the corner.

Silk, who had never been caught, who never would be, stood with the policeman's hand on her shoulder. His other hand was reaching for handcuffs. In Silk's hands was the small bejewelled tortoise, the word 'VITA' picked out on the shell.

CHAPTER FIFTEEN

Arkady was struggling. Silk, of all of them, was supposed to be indestructible. Arkady's voice strained so hard to be cheerful it came out three octaves higher than usual. 'She'll be fine! I mean, she can pick any lock! So she'll be fine, right?'

They had run, all three of them, once it was obvious it was useless to stay; they had left Silk in the hands of the law. They stopped outside Carnegie Hall. Pain and shame and breathlessness had made Vita's face turn scarlet, and she rounded on him now. 'How is she going to be fine? Don't say stupid things just to make yourself feel better.'

'Don't call me stupid for hoping our friend is all right!'

'Don't fight.' Samuel spoke quietly, but there was ferocity in his voice. 'We don't have time to fight. We don't have any time at all. Vita only means Silk doesn't have tools.'

'Exactly! She's wearing that stupid coat – she doesn't even have a hairpin. She can't pick a lock with her fingers.'

'Fine.' Arkady scowled at Vita. 'We'll get some tools to her. Simple!'

'How are we going to do that? We don't even know where she is! There must be dozens of police cells she could be in!'

'I know where she is,' said Samuel.

'How?'

'I saw the serial number on his badge. I know which police station he belongs to.'

'How on earth do you know that?'

'My uncle always said it pays for us to know the

ways of the police: ever since I was a tiny kid. She'll be in Brooklyn.'

'Well, let's go then!' said Arkady. 'What are you waiting for?'

'We have to have a plan,' said Vita. Arkady stared at her, but she sat down on the kerb and began to spin her penknife around her fingers, her jaw set with angry concentration. 'This isn't the circus. This is serious. This is *real*.'

'I know that.' Arkady sat down next to her. His shoulders were hunched, and he scrubbed at his face with his sleeve. 'I do take it seriously. I take *her* seriously.'

Vita glanced at him and saw with a jolt that his face looked ancient: haggard and old and weary. With gut-deep effort, she forced a small smile. 'Sorry,' she said. 'I know.'

The minutes passed. And slowly, very slowly, Arkady's face began to transform, until it looked thirteen years old again.

'Can I say something?' he said.

Vita winced. 'You don't have to ask. I'm sorry, I—'

Arkady interrupted. 'Listen, then – I've got a question.'

'What?'

'The tweezers in your penknife – are they shiny?'

A crow flew in through the front door of the police station the next morning as calmly as if it were coming in to report a missing package.

Arkady, who had carried the crow on a streetcar down to the Brooklyn Bridge, stroking and crooning to her all the way so she wouldn't take flight, cast her in through the doorway. He whispered, 'Good luck! *Ydachi!*' and ducked out.

The bird alighted on the desk, and for a split second, nothing happened.

Then someone began to scream. 'Get it out! Get it out, it's unlucky!'

'Don't be stupid, that's magpies!'

'I don't care, it's filthy! They carry diseases!'

The policeman behind the desk took a great swipe at it, and the bird took off. She swiftly became affronted and confused. Crows, when affronted, are apt to dive-bomb the nearest living thing, and soon pandemonium reigned.

Silk sat on the bare bed of the barred cell she had spent the night in. She radiated despair. At the shrieks, she looked up, and saw the bird.

Her black feathers stirred a memory, and Silk's eyes widened.

Silk approached the bars, a slow and steady presence in a room of screaming and flailing. And Silk, who remembered everything she saw, who memorised the faces on the street so she never robbed them twice, remembered the crow's name.

'Rimsky!' she called, and the bird, harried now and panicking, swooped towards her, her beak still clamped around her prize. Silk stretched her arm out through the bars of her prison. The bird landed on it and dropped her cargo, nipping at her thumb before taking off again.

Silk winced. Bird affection, she thought, was a painful thing.

Eventually the panic died down, and Rimsky was

caught in a tea towel and cast ignominiously into the street.

Nobody saw Silk slip something silver-grey into her stocking, and sit back, quiet and hunched and dejected, in the corner of her cell. She unplaited her hair, and let it fall, a protective curtain, over her eyes.

It was a good thing nobody saw her face. Because, try as she might to disguise it, Silk radiated hope. All that Friday afternoon and night, Silk radiated waiting, and *hush*, and *count-down*.

At last, as the clock struck three in the morning, the officer on duty laid his head down on his folded arms for an illicit nap. Silk slipped the tweezers out of her woollen stocking, twisted them four, five, six times in the lock, and crept on soundless feet towards the door.

A man in the cell next door, ex-army, ex-almost-everything now, with soot in his nails and a dog on a string, saw her go, but he only rose to stand, snapped to attention, and raised one hand in a salute he hadn't used for many years. And Silk returned the salute, as she slipped out into the New York night.

*

That night the city was swept by a premature winter. An ice snap froze the water in the pipes. Sleet washed down the city, swept the detritus of the mud and old newspaper and furious cats out from murky alleyways into the main roads.

And through the hail and sleet, glaring defiantly at the weather, came a lone figure, its shoulders hunched against the cold, walking towards Carnegie Hall.

Up in Vita's apartment, Samuel, Arkady and Vita sat in her bedroom, their eyes on the clock, waiting. Vita's mother had blinked slightly at the sight of the two boys, but had agreed, rather than send them home in the dark, to let them spend the night in the sitting room.

'It's nice that you've made some friends,' she had said to Vita. 'Next time give me a little more warning.'

Vita was just about to give up hope when the window began to intrude on her consciousness. It didn't open; it didn't become any less dark outside – but the darkness seemed to be watching her. It made itself suddenly felt.

She crossed and looked out. On the street below stood a figure, her long blonde plait drenched to grey in the rain.

The figure grinned up at her.

'I came to drop off your tweezers,' called Silk.

Ten minutes later, all four children were sitting on Vita's bed, and Silk was eating a sandwich made of everything sweet Vita could find – butter, peanut butter, honey, chocolate shavings, and a sliced banana. Vita had suggested adding ketchup, but Silk had refused.

'So,' said Silk, 'tomorrow's Saturday. Are we still on? We go tomorrow?'

'I'm still in,' said Samuel.

'So am I,' said Arkady. 'Of course!'

They looked at Vita, their faces alight. They could have powered a factory, so brightly did they shine.

Vita looked at the red book in her hand. It felt far heavier than the paper it contained. She weighed the secret she had been carrying around in her chest since she had met Silk. She made a decision.

'Listen,' she said. 'There's something I've not told you …'

And she spread the book out in front of them, and began to explain, carefully, meticulously, the final part of the plan.

CHAPTER SIXTEEN

'So: 10.45 p.m. at Grand Central Station, near the coffee stall?' said Silk. Her face was as unreadable as ever, but her breath came quicker than usual. The two girls had woken early the next morning, having slept head to toe in Vita's narrow bed.

'Like sisters,' Silk had said. Neither had the cleanest feet; neither had minded.

'Yes. The last train out is 11.02,' said Vita. 'But there's one final thing I have to do.'

Silk nodded. 'I know. We'll see you at the station,'

and she went into the sitting room to wake Samuel and Arkady.

Bile rose in Vita's throat, but she forced it down. *This is not the time to be afraid*, she told herself. *You can be afraid later, when it's over.*

That evening, Vita approached the Dakota slowly. She had wrapped her coat tight around herself, but it gave little protection against the cold, and none at all against the fear.

She had known she would be followed, and she was. She had been counting on it.

She did not turn round to see who it was, only registering the shadowy figure following her down the pavement. She stayed in the brightest streets, amid the widest crowds. They wouldn't touch her in such a public place.

It was 9 p.m. The lights of Sorrotore's apartment were off. She set her jaw and tucked her hair behind her ears. The red book was rolled up in her coat pocket; she carried a cloth bag on her back with a collection of trowels clanking against her spine. She wore her blue dress, unfamiliar and tight around the shoulders. She was ready.

She would be quick, as quick as her feet would go.

The desk clerk at the Dakota looked up at the girl in front of him without interest.

'Excuse me,' she said, 'but is Mr Victor Sorrotore in this evening?'

'He's dining with the young Rockefellers. You want to leave a message?'

Vita shook her head. So Sorrotore was definitely in New York; definitely not up on the Hudson river.

She walked slowly out of the building, her eyes sharp, searching every face she saw. She stepped on to the street. One second she was crossing the road; the next, a hand grabbed her shoulder, and pulled her round to face a man in a brown suit and hat and blue tie.

'Hey, you.'

It was Dillinger.

Vita screamed. Instinct kicked at her solar plexus and it came out of her mouth without her permission, a shrill, thin shriek that surprised her. She screamed again, deliberately this time, and a woman with a vast coif of hair and a vast green handbag stopped and turned.

'Shut up!' hissed Dillinger. 'I'm not going to hurt you – the boss just wants his signet ring back.' There was a pleading look in his eyes. His fingers dug into her collarbone. 'Come on, kid. I need this!'

She twisted. 'Let *go*!'

Dillinger hung on. His eyes were hot. 'The boss'll forgive me! He will, if I give him that ring! You don't understand—'

She ducked her chin and bit, hard, at his hand. Then she darted to the right, into an oncoming crowd of tourists carrying red guidebooks, and ran, as fast as her left leg would take her, counting on the crowd to slow him down.

'Stop her!' cried Dillinger. 'Stop that girl! Thief!'

She glanced round. He was charging after her, and people, seeing his smart suit and elegant hat, were parting to let him through.

Vita turned a sharp left, on to a great bustling street. She careened head first into a man absorbed in his newspaper as he walked.

She thought about dashing into one of the great shining department stores that lined the street, but those would be conspicuous places for a running child. A crossing light turned green, and she thrust herself into the centre of the crowd as it strode across the street.

At the far side she hesitated, looking to the left and right. She took in a great gasp of air, and went on.

Her breath was becoming ragged, and her left foot was on fire, sending shooting pains up the whole left side of her body. She used the street lamps to propel herself forward, grabbing them and thrusting herself on. She tried to think as she ran.

She limped past a sign: SUBWAY. A sudden memory came to her. The turnstile, where people fed it their tokens; it worked like a revolving door, but there was a space, underneath: wide enough for a child, too narrow for an adult.

She stumbled down the steps, looking over her shoulder to see if he was following. The steps were wet, and she almost slipped, clutching at the arm of a woman with two children of Vita's age, who stared after her. 'Someone's in a hurry for their bedtime story,' said the mother, and the children laughed.

Behind her came thundering steps. Vita didn't let herself stop to think; didn't let herself measure the gap between the turnstile and the floor. She pushed to the front of the crowd, ignoring the yelps and angry coughs and the call of 'Oh, for heaven's sake!' from one grey-haired man, and dived, head first, on to the floor, which was muddy and wet, sliding on the slick surface under the gate and pulling her left foot clear just as one of the subway officials made a grab for her shoes.

She scrambled to her feet, ignoring the pain and the blood on her palm from the fall, and hurtled down the stairs. The crowd closed around her, and she became invisible.

A train was just pulling into the platform. Vita stepped on to it, and stood, her heart thundering. She did not look back. It took all the willpower in her bones to keep facing straight ahead, her hands in her pockets, her heart pounding.

Had she looked back, she would have seen Dillinger bend to pick up what she had dropped.

She would have seen him turn the notebook over in his hands, and the glint of its soft red cover glow against the grey of the darkening night.

CHAPTER SEVENTEEN

Grand Central Station was almost empty. Rush hour had passed, leaving only the smell of raincoats and spilt coffee. The ceiling, painted with stars, shone down on wet floors and a few shivering homeless men, sitting in a corner.

Vita stood under Orion's Belt, in a pool of light, waiting. She had straightened her dress, wiped the dirt from a patch by her hip, and brushed her hair with her fingers. Her heart pounded with each footstep she heard. Every time a head came into view, she flinched. She had the cloth bag slung over one shoulder.

The time ticked by, remorseless. Vita wrapped her fingers more tightly around the four tickets she had bought from the uninterested young man in the ticket booth. Her other hand clutched the bundle of hard-saved dollars in her coat pocket. It would get them from the station to the house and back again.

'Eight minutes to eleven,' she whispered. 'Ten minutes until the train goes. That's ages.'

At 10.54, she looked again at her watch; and at 10.55, and 10.58. Four minutes to go. What were they *doing*? The cold in the station seeped into her stomach, but Vita whispered to herself, '*Give them one more minute.*'

And even as the words left her mouth, she heard a sound that made her heart leap. Running footsteps thundered through the almost empty hall, and a girl and two boys, the girl's plait flying horizontally behind her, came sprinting over the smooth stone floor.

'We're here!' called Arkady, as if she could have missed them.

'Nearly … got caught,' panted Silk.

'My father … almost saw us,' said Arkady, doubled over.

'Discuss later!' said Samuel. He carried a bag across one shoulder. 'Two minutes!'

'Platform seven!' said Vita.

Her foot still throbbed from her sprint earlier that night, and she could not keep up with the others. An unexpected crowd of late-night commuters came out from the station café as they went past, and Vita was jostled by a tall boy running the opposite way. She dodged sideways, and he stepped the same way – then again, the boy hissing with frustration, the other way – then he looped around her and was gone. His hat was pulled low over his eyes, but he grinned as he darted off, and his grin was familiar.

She stumbled on to the platform, but the train was making alarming noises – *get-ready*, *get-go* noises – and as she limped up, her hand almost close enough to touch the black shining paint, it began to move.

211

The others were already on the train. Arkady's face in the window was a mask of horror.

Vita had no time to feel anything, no despair, nothing. Samuel's face disappeared from the window … and suddenly the door of the last carriage on the train flew open, and a long arm reached out.

A porter on the platform shouted, 'Hey! Stop that!' and Vita half jumped, half fell forwards.

Her hand closed on Samuel's, he shouted, '*Hep!*' and she was heaved on to the floor of the train. The door slammed shut behind her. The porter on the platform, who was young, with the feeble traces of an unsuccessful beard, put his tongue out at them and made a rude gesture.

'Thank you!' said Vita, and Samuel grinned.

'We couldn't leave without you. You're the *just-in-case*.'

They found Arkady and Silk sitting two in a row on the bench-seat of a small compartment. Samuel and Vita dropped on to the padded bench opposite. All of the others, she saw, wore their disguises.

The collector entered, took their tickets, nodded

approvingly at Silk's sweet smile, at their general spruceness, and moved on. And the train thundered on through the night, away from the city and towards the unknown.

They pulled into the train station deep in the pitch-black night. Mist hung low on the ground, and they clambered out on to the dimly lit platform, stamping their feet to wake up their toes.

Nobody else got off, and there were no porters. The station was no more than a single platform, a stationmaster's lodge, and the darkness of the countryside stretching away in every direction. A horse coughed and neighed nearby.

'Where now?' asked Arkady.

Vita put the return tickets in Samuel's hand. 'You look after these, OK? We'll get the station cab to take us – Grandpa used to tell me about the cab driver. He's very old, and he sleeps above the station.'

'Will he mind being woken?'

'Not if we pay him double. I've saved up all my dollars. We won't ask him to take us all the way – we'll walk the last bit.' She saw their eyes glance, in unison, down to her leg. 'I'll be fine.'

She put her hand into her coat pocket.

There was nothing there.

She tried the other pocket. 'The money ...' she muttered. She began to turn the pockets out.

Silk was immediately alert. 'What money?'

'The money for the taxi!'

'Are you sure it was in your coat pocket?'

'Positive!' And then the memory flared up. 'That boy! There was a boy in the station – he jostled me! He was one of those boys, that day in the alley!'

'Did he do a two-step? Left, and then right – and make a face like it was your fault?'

'Yes!' said Vita. And then, as the full horror of what this meant sunk in, 'He's a pickpocket, then?'

'His name's Fergus. He's got a black hole where his conscience should be. I'll kill him when we get back!'

'Can we walk instead?' asked Samuel.

'Not before sunrise,' said Vita. 'It would take hours. We'd never get there in time.'

'So what do we do?' Arkady turned to her. His eyes were too trusting to meet full on.

Vita shivered. She suddenly felt very small, and very young, and very foolish – just a schoolgirl in the middle of nowhere, with a handful of storybook delusions.

The horse neighed again, and it sounded like a mocking laugh.

But Arkady's face suddenly broke into a grin. 'Horses!' he said. He turned to Samuel. 'Can you hear that?'

Samuel caught Arkady's meaning instantly; he turned, listened. 'There's two!'

Arkady began to run towards the sound. 'It's probably a mare – quite old, from the whinny – let's hope not too old to ride!'

So they left the pool of light of the station, and went, half sprinting, half groping, into the dark. Vita pulled the torch from her coat and shone it ahead of them. The road was paved but weathered, with potholes deep enough to twist an ankle in.

The horses were in a field looking on to the road, two dark blurs in the night. The gate was rusty, sealed with a vicious twist of barbed wire, but Arkady, Silk and Samuel cleared it at a jump, and Vita clambered carefully after them.

The horses smelt them coming and took off, neighing high and scared, to the far corner of the field. Samuel and Arkady exchanged glances.

'Do you want help?' asked Samuel.

Arkady shook his head. 'Easier just them and me.' He left the pool of light cast by the torch and went, sure-footed over the grass, following the noise and smell. Vita heard his whisper on the wind, '*Ne boisya*. Don't be scared.'

The three waited, huddled close but not quite touching in a corner of the field, trying not to listen to the strange rustlings in the dark trees above them. The cold was insidious; it crept into every pore of Vita's skin. There was a sudden sharp whinny in the dark, and an answering murmur in Russian.

Then there was a laugh of delight, and a thump, and into the pool of light rode the boy, sitting high on a black horse. Behind came a bay mare. They had no tack, no reins, but they responded to Arkady's every call and touch.

'Let's go,' said Arkady, 'before someone comes.'

Samuel crossed to the mare and stroked her. 'She's strong,' he said admiringly. 'She'll be fast.'

Silk was looking in horror at the horses. 'I didn't realise they'd be so big!' she said.

'You've never seen a horse?' asked Arkady. He sounded, in the dark, horrified.

'Of course I have!' Silk's voice was shrill. 'But not up close!'

'Then why are you scared? Are you allergic?'

She took a deep breath, and her old sardonic voice tried to restore itself. 'Normal people aren't rich enough to know if they're allergic to horses. They're just … big, is all.'

Arkady held out his hands, cupped, at the side of the horse. 'Put your foot here and swing up – it's far easier than climbing a drainpipe.'

'Drainpipes don't bite,' said Silk, but she put her foot in his hands and he propelled her, with only a little scrambling, on to the mare's back. She sat hunched, her fur-trimmed white coat bulging at the front.

It took some work, and a lot of help from Arkady,

for Vita to clamber on to the other horse's back, but for once she barely registered it. The swing and buzz and hope of the mission had come back in a burst that warmed her veins, as Arkady leaped up in front of her. Then Samuel was up on the mare, and they were facing the fence that separated them from the road.

'Who first?' asked Arkady, and, 'Together,' said Samuel – and without warning the horses were charging at the posts.

'Grip with your knees!' called Arkady, and suddenly Vita was flying over the gate, tipping so far back she was at right angles to the ground, and then the horses landed, clattering, on the deserted country road.

'Where?' asked Arkady, his voice low.

'That way,' said Vita. She pulled the map out of her coat pocket, and shone her battery torch at it, just to be sure. But she knew it by heart: she had looked at it a thousand times. 'Follow that star,' she said.

CHAPTER EIGHTEEN

Vita's torch cast shadows through the trees, giving the branches elbows and hands and guns. Arkady whistled a tune, but the sound was thin and piping, deadened by the weight of the forest overhead, and he stopped at a look from Silk. Vita turned up her coat collar, and they rode on in grim silence.

Finally the trees began to thin. Beyond the forest were wild meadows, unfarmed and untouched, and then muddy sandbank, and the sound of the river.

'We'd better leave the horses here, in the wood,' said Vita. 'They'll attract attention.'

She swung down on to the ground. It was further than she'd judged, and she landed hard, skinning one knee. She thought of her grandfather's long, strong fingers, wrapping bandages around her scrapes when she was young, and scrambled to her feet.

Arkady slid to the earth as easily as if stepping out of bed, and offered his hand to Silk. To everyone's surprise – including her own, from the look on Silk's face – she took it.

Arkady led the horses a few yards back into the forest, looking for somewhere that provided grazing. They came at the click of his tongue.

'Shouldn't we tie them?' said Silk.

'What with?' said Arkady.

'Can't you – I don't know – tie something round their necks?' said Silk.

'They'll wait,' said Arkady. 'I know them, now.'

'Which way?' asked Samuel. Three pairs of eyes turned to Vita.

'This way,' she said, leading the way out of the

trees. 'Wait a second, the moon's coming out from behind that cloud. There! Hudson Castle!'

The eyes followed the direction of her hand.

'Ah,' said Silk. 'You weren't exaggerating when you said "Castle".'

It looked like it had been designed by someone who had seen more castles in picture books than in the flesh; it looked like someone had sought the essence of *castle*.

The ornamental lake was edged with trees, the water blue-black. Rising on stone foundations from the middle of the water was a wall, and beyond the wall a garden, surrounding on three sides a great block of brick and stone.

The castle was topped with a single turret and battlements, silver-black in the moonlight. One wall of the castle dropped straight into the water, and its reflection glinted and shimmered, fairy-tale-like. Vita's whole body thrilled and shook at the sight of it. It was real.

'My great-great-great-grandfather saw it in France,' said Vita. 'He knocked it down, and rebuilt it here; it came out a bit wonky, actually: the turret's falling down. Everyone said he was mad, but he said, if that was true, at least he'd be mad in a castle, and they'd be sane in a house.'

'Where's the boat?' asked Samuel.

'Hidden under a willow tree, to the west side of the lake. It's called *Lizzy*, after my grandmother.'

'What if Sorrotore found the boat and sold it?' said Silk.

'It wouldn't be worth anything,' said Vita. 'It's so old.'

'Well then, what if it leaks?'

'There's no point in fighting about a possibly non-existent boat,' said Samuel. 'Let's go and see.'

They ran in single file towards the lake, the long grass jabbing at Vita's knees through the material of her dress. They startled two rabbits, who took off across the wild grass.

'It's so quiet,' said Silk. 'I've never been anywhere so quiet in my life.'

But even as she spoke, a noise tore through the air, rough and high and angry. Barking.

'That'll be the guard dogs,' said Vita. She looked at Arkady, whose eyes were narrowed.

'German Shepherds,' he said. 'Two years old, maybe two and a half. Probably both male.' The bark came again. 'They've not been properly cared for – can you hear the scratch in the second one's voice? It's had an infection that wasn't treated. So they'll probably be hungry.'

The boat was exactly where Grandpa said it had always been.

They reached the edge of the lake, listening for human voices, and Vita crawled through the shrubby trees that grew along the muddy shore, skirting the thorn bushes as best she could in the dark, until she reached the wooden canoe.

Grandpa had said it was bright green, the colour of Lizzy's eyes. In fact, the paint had peeled so much that it was mostly brownish grey, but there were places where the colour still lingered. Vita picked off one of the splinters of paint and put it in her pocket.

The other three came running in a doubled-up crouch. They ran like what they were – a collection of acrobats and thieves – and their feet were completely silent across the muddy sand. They gathered round the boat and pushed it into the water.

Silk glanced over her shoulder. 'And you're sure there's no nightwatchman?'

Vita shook her head. 'I don't think so.'

'You don't *think*?'

'Why would there be? There's the guard, but he sleeps in a cottage on the other side of the lake. At night there're just the dogs.'

The barking came again, deep and rough-edged.

'Oh good,' said Silk.

There was a brief scuffle over who should row. Silk solved the matter by seizing an oar and brandishing it like a sword while Vita grabbed the other. At first they both splashed haplessly in the water – '*Shh!*' hissed Arkady – but then they got into the rhythm of it, and they moved almost silently across the glass surface of the lake.

Samuel sat in the stern of the boat, looking up at the vast brick wall as they drew closer and closer. The map had showed a small landing jetty round the other side of the lake, but it was in full sight of the care-taker's cottage; instead they rowed straight at the garden wall that rose, looming, out of the water.

'Apparently,' said Vita, 'my great-great-great-grand-father saw the houses in Venice, which drop straight into the canal, and thought it was the most beautiful thing he'd ever seen, like a woman rising from a lake, he said. So he got his engineers to—'

'Can we save the architectural history for the train home?' said Silk between clenched teeth, hauling on the oar.

They were close to the wall now. It was built of large grey bricks, rough-hewn and well cemented.

'Here?' asked Samuel.

'I think so,' said Vita. And then, trying to sound more certain, 'Yes, exactly here.'

Samuel stood up in the boat, barely rocking it. The carefully blank politeness with which he faced the world had vanished. His eyes were growing wild and fierce, and the edges of his mouth were beginning to twitch.

Arkady turned to Samuel. 'I don't see how you're going to—'

But Samuel shook his head, holding up a hand for silence. Behind his eyes were six dozen calculations. His lips moved as he murmured under his breath, and his fingers quivered by his sides. He reached into his bag and pulled out a rope; it was a huge, heavy coil.

'No grappling hook?' said Arkady. 'I thought you'd have a hook on the end of it?'

'The wall's too thick,' said Samuel. 'I'm doing it my way.'

He pulled off his shoes, tied the rope twice around his waist, then looped the remainder over his shoulder, the movement making the boat rock under him. Vita reached out and tried to grasp the wall, but there was nowhere for her hands to gain purchase.

'OK,' he said. 'Keep the boat still.' He leaned over, reached up to the wall and pushed his fingers into the gap between two bricks.

'Samuel!' said Arkady. His voice was suddenly full of panic. 'Don't! It's not possible to climb a sheer brick wall!'

It is not possible to climb a sheer brick wall. It is not possible – unless you grew up climbing as close to the sky as you can get. It is not possible, unless you decided at the age of five that you would fly and spent the rest of your life finding a way to do so.

Samuel reached higher up, and his fingers found another gap, digging in against the mortar. He pulled himself up, his feet scrabbling against the stone. Steadily, silently, he rose.

Vita sat frozen to the spot, her eyes prickling, her breath shaking with the skill of it. It was Arkady who got to his feet, unsteadily, to stand underneath his friend, arms half outstretched. Vita and Silk stood too, and they waited, ready to catch him when, as he surely must, he fell.

But Samuel was nearing the top, and he was moving fast now; astonishingly fast. One arm swung up over the top of the wall, there was a gasping, heaving noise, and suddenly there was a boy in neat grey trousers and the look of an aristocrat sitting astride the bricks. He settled himself with one leg dangling either side, and lay the front of his body flat against the top of the wall. Then he let the rope cascade down to the boat.

'Come on up!' he whispered. 'Vita first. It's her wall.'

Vita shook her head, and felt the flush in her cheeks. She had, secretly, been dreading this moment. It was dark, but even so she did not want them to watch her struggle with the rope. 'I'll go last. I'll take longest.'

Silk spoke quietly in the dark, and there was no sarcasm in her voice. 'We'll wait,' she said.

Vita's hands were wet with sweat. She grasped the rope, found her grip suddenly slippery and unreliable. She wound her right foot in the rope, and used her left foot to press upwards, ignoring the cry of pain in her Achilles tendon. She reached up, seized a spot above her head, and hauled herself up a few inches.

'Good,' said Samuel. 'Unwind your right foot, and do it all again. Just six inches. Don't think about yards – think about inches.'

The wind blew her hair in her eyes and mouth as she climbed. She didn't look down, but up, at Samuel's beckoning face, hauling herself hand over hand. He half dragged her up the last foot, and she sat, upright on the wall.

'Now Silk,' said Samuel.

Silk's hands were quick, but her legs were long and awkward, and she glared at Arkady below her when he offered help. It was as she reached the top, and Vita and Samuel were pulling her up to sit alongside them, that the barking rent the air.

A dark shadow came tearing across the grass towards them.

CHAPTER NINETEEN

The rope tightened, and Arkady's head appeared, like a jack-in-the-box, at the top of the wall. He nodded to Samuel; the two understood each other without words. Arkady heaved the rope up one side of the wall and dropped it down the other; Samuel braced himself, and Arkady grabbed the rope and slid down it, wincing as the rope burned his hands.

The dogs were almost on him. They were German Shepherds, one brown and grey and one solid black, both tall as Arkady's shoulder and moving fast. The black one was closest, and its teeth were so white and so many that they seemed to precede the dog itself by several inches.

Arkady swallowed, and for one second his smile faltered, but then he forced it back, determinedly, and stepped towards the dogs, one hand outstretched towards the open jaws. He whispered in Russian as he went.

The dogs halted. The black dog stood, growling, two paces from Arkady. Its hackles rose along its back. Arkady continued to talk, and he added his whistle – the whistle that could summon a murder of crows out of a neighbouring rooftop. The brown dog whined, and the black dog's growl became less sure of itself. Arkady stepped closer, palm held upwards.

Too close. The black dog snapped at it in earnest and gave a sudden volley of barks. Vita closed her eyes in one long, bleak blink of horror.

'*Nyet!*' said Arkady sternly. '*Ya znayu, ty ne takoi.* I know you're better than that.' And he whistled, again, long and low, and laid one hand on each of the dogs' noses.

When Vita opened her eyes, the black dog was lying on its side, and Arkady was kneeling at its head, rubbing it between the ears, while the other tried to lick the inside of his sleeve.

He looked at the collars. 'This one's Viking, and this one's Hunter. You can come down. Don't burn your hands on the rope.'

They crouched, hidden among bushes, looking out at the garden. It was huge, and ornate, though it had run wild now, and there was ivy growing everywhere they looked. Paths stretched in every direction from the back door of the house, some of them small and winding around flower beds, some lined with gravel. A small walled garden lay on the west side of the lawn, an array of rose beds to the east. The last winter roses were still hanging from the bushes, overblown but still a strange, bloody midnight red in the moonlight, intermingled with creepers.

'I can't see the fountain,' whispered Silk.

'No,' said Vita. 'It's in the walled garden – over there, see?'

They crossed over the lawn, Viking following Arkady adoringly and Hunter's tail wagging against the boy's leg.

Silk glanced across the lawn at the back door. 'Is that the door with the unpickable lock?' she whispered.

'Yes,' said Vita. She looked at the house, rising up and up into the night sky. 'They all are. It's a fortress.' Vita reached the walled garden ahead of the others. There was a small black wooden door in the wall, just as the plans had shown. She pushed it. It was locked.

A hand moved her aside.

'Let me,' whispered Silk. She slipped her length of wire into the lock. 'It's not an easy one. Just a second.'

It took her less than a minute, but each second felt like a week. Silk let out a hiss of relief as the lock clicked open.

They filed in, Hunter and Viking barging among them, and closed the door behind them.

Vita's breath came out in a great wave of relief.

'What now?' said Arkady.

Vita gestured at the fountain. It stood dry, but the skeletons of roses grew up high around it. Age had chipped away at its beauty, but had not destroyed it: it was a statue of a laughing boy. The boy looked, Vita thought, a lot like her grandfather might have, once. She pulled her trowel out of the bag. 'We dig,' she said.

They began to dig in earnest. The ground was icy, and soon Vita's hands were numb. But she shovelled and shovelled, her trowel occasionally clashing against Silk's, and all of them were soon filthy up to the elbow.

The hole grew bigger. Six inches deep … a foot deep.

Vita felt her blood speed faster and faster through her body. *Would it work? Would the plan work?*

And then it came. Footsteps, running. The others dropped their trowels and jumped to their feet, but Vita kept hold of hers, and moved to stand, ready, in front of her friends.

The wooden door in the stone wall flew open, and a man came bursting through, sweating and panting and contorted with anger.

234

'What the hell's all this?' The guard was tall and wide, and there was nothing kind in his face.

Vita didn't let herself hesitate. She charged straight at the man, her trowel held out in front of her like a bayonet. She felt his arm catch her across the shoulder, and tripped sideways, spinning to hit out at his chest. She felt both his hands close on her upper arm.

'Run!' called Vita. She turned to the others, who stood straight-backed, clench-fisted, watching.

'I mean it!' she cried, and a sudden white-hot panic rose in her.

They had to run.

'What are you doing? *You swore you'd run!*'

But they didn't run.

And now the guard was gripping her wrist with an agonising grasp and was reaching out to catch Samuel, who stood there, unmoving.

'No!' said Vita. 'This isn't the plan! *Run!* We had a pact! *RUN!*'

A second man appeared and stood in front of the door.

'Stand still,' he said, and pointed a rifle at Silk's heart. 'Don't move, or there'll be an accident.'

They were led in single file up through the garden, across the lawn, through the back door, with the rifle bringing up the rear. The windows were all barred in thick, ugly, black-painted iron.

The kitchen door was bolted from the inside; the guard went round and unbolted it. Vita saw Silk looking from out of the corner of her eye at the locks.

Silk shook her head. 'It really is a fortress,' she whispered.

Vita held her bag tight under her coat; nobody had yet demanded it.

They were led through an empty kitchen, painted a bright cobalt blue, then down a hallway to a wooden door, which opened on to stone steps and a large wine cellar.

The cellar was open at the bottom of the steps, and then stretched away in aisles of shelves, a library of wine bottles, a few shelves of whisky, one or two of rum. Someone had been tasting them recently, and a few half-drunk bottles stood on a shelf near the stairs.

Those are my grandfather's, not Sorrotore's, thought Vita, and a further surge of anger rose in her. *Thief.*

The floor was of stone slabs. There was no light.

The guard pushed the four children until they were standing with their backs against the wall of the cellar. Then, still pointing the rifle, both men retreated.

The door closed, and Vita turned to stare at the three faces in front of her. She was breathless, desperate, but they only stood, waiting for her to speak, Arkady smiling slightly.

'Why didn't you run?' she asked. The words were strangled; her chest was thumping hard enough to choke her.

Arkady grinned. 'You never thought we were actually going to, did you?' And he laughed.

Samuel smiled his odd, hidden half-smile. 'We never actually promised.'

'Think back,' said Silk, 'to what we *actually* said.'

CHAPTER TWENTY

The Night Before

Vita had sat on the bed, in her room, high up above New York, and told them the truth. She had spread out the book in front of them.

'There's one last thing I have to do,' she said.

'What?'

'I have to get this book to Sorrotore. I have to give him The Plan.'

Three sets of eyes, aghast, bewildered, stared back at her.

'But then he'll know where to find the emerald!'

'No,' said Vita. She sighed so hard her ribs creaked, and the sigh had all the secrets she had been keeping in it. 'He won't.'

'He will!' said Arkady. 'Look, right here! The book says—'

Vita looked out across the city, towards the Dakota. 'The book is a lie.'

The eyes watching her widened, then narrowed.

'What?' Silk edged away from Vita. 'You've been lying to us?'

'The emerald isn't in the fountain,' said Vita. 'But I need him to believe it is. I need him to put all his attention, all his men, all his focus, on that fountain.'

'So where *is* the emerald?' said Samuel.

'It's in the house.'

'But you said the house can't be—'

'Can't be broken into,' said Vita. 'Exactly.'

'It said so in the newspaper!' said Arkady.

'I know,' said Vita.

'So it's impossible!' said Silk.

'Impossible doesn't mean it's not worth doing. What I need to do is get caught.'

'Get caught?' Silk and Samuel spoke together.

'There are no houses for miles. If I get caught, there's only one place where they could keep me until the police arrive.'

Samuel's mouth formed an 'O' of sudden comprehension. 'In the house?'

'Exactly. I can't break in – but they can let me in.'

'But the red book!' said Arkady. 'It had all the plans in it – all the detail! The blueprint! Everything said it was in the fountain!'

'That's because I didn't write it for me. I wrote it for Sorrotore.'

'But if the house is impossible to break into, it's impossible to break out of! So we'll all be stuck there!' said Arkady.

'No!' said Vita. 'No – twice no! It's not impossible to break out of. And no, you won't be stuck there – because you'll run. You won't be there.'

'No we won't!' said Arkady.

'You will. You have to promise you will. You'll run

240

out and away. I need you to help me get as far as the walled garden, and I might need you to help me start the hole, so it looks real – but then I need you to run. You can get the cab to wait and take you back to the station, and be home in time for breakfast. And I'll search the house alone.'

'Why didn't you tell us this before?' said Silk. Her eyes were still and wary.

'I was afraid to,' said Vita, and she could feel her eyes burning. 'I thought … I thought, once I said it out loud, it would be over. I thought you might all say it's ridiculous. Too difficult – too stupid – too dangerous.' Then she drew a breath, and told them the shameful, selfish truth. 'I thought if I told you right away, you'd say no.'

Arkady let out a snort of indignation. 'I would *never* say something's too dangerous!'

'I know,' said Vita. It was an effort to speak. 'I didn't know you then. I do now.'

'So all of it – you've had this planned, all along?'

She nodded. 'Planning – watching, thinking – it's what I do.'

Samuel looked at Vita; at the longing written in her hands and feet, at her frown.

'All right,' he said. 'I'm still in, if the others are.'

Silk took one slow, hard look at Vita. Then she nodded. 'It was always crazy. It's still crazy. I'm still in.'

'So you'll run, when the guards come? You swear you'll run?' said Vita. 'Like Samuel said – when one of us says run, we have to run. It's the pact.'

And they had all nodded.

'I'll get some more cocoa,' said Vita, and set out towards the kitchen.

Arkady looked at Silk, and Silk looked at Samuel.

Arkady held out his left hand: the fingers were crossed. 'I'm not running,' he said.

Samuel nodded. He took his hands out of his pockets. All of his fingers were crossed. He smiled his half-smile. The two boys turned to Silk.

'I didn't cross my fingers,' she said, and grinned. 'I just lied. I'm not running anywhere.'

CHAPTER TWENTY-ONE

The cellar was icy and dark, but when Vita shivered it was not with cold. She reached into her bag and pulled out the torch – the battery was very low now, and so it cast only a faint glow, but it was better than nothing – and the two half-burned candles she had stowed there. She flicked a match with her thumb-nail – a trick her grandfather had taught her – and, for once, it lit. She looked at the faces in front of her.

'Why didn't you tell me you weren't going to run?' she said.

'Would you have brought us with you, if we told you?' said Samuel.

'No,' said Vita. 'Of course not.'

'Well then,' said Silk.

'We're a troupe now,' said Arkady. 'We fought together; we ate together. We're a crew.'

Vita felt the warmth of it spread up her stomach to her face. But before she could speak, the lock on the door crunched, and the door opened a crack. 'Don't be doing anything stupid. Sorrotore said to say he's in the motorboat. He'll be here soon enough.'

Vita's heart jolted. 'What motorboat?' she whispered.

But the door slammed shut. Four faces stared at each other.

'Sorrotore can't come here!' said Vita. 'That's not the plan! He was just supposed to tell the men where to dig! So they'd be distracted, and I could search the house. And that's why we came by the last train – so he can't follow! It would take hours and hours longer to drive.' Her voice was very small. 'I didn't think of a motorboat.'

The dark house, in the middle of the dark lake, she could face. The shotgun, she could face. But Sorrotore – his smile, and his eyes, and the power that he wore like cloth laid across his shoulders – she had not counted on that. All the remaining strength in her leg gave way, and she sat down on the floor.

'There's nothing we can do about it now,' said Silk. She reached inside her white swan-feather cloak and drew out a small cloth bag. She dumped it open, and a flash of bright cloth, silk and wool, came tumbling out.

'Here. If we're going to do this – and, Vita, we *are*, and you can't stop us – I thought we should be dressed in the way that makes sense to us. I packed your clothes while you were washing this morning.'

'My sweater!' said Arkady.

There was scuffling in the dark.

Arkady's sweater glowed deep scarlet in the candle-light. Samuel flexed his arms in his black singlet, his black cotton trousers skimming the ground. Both boys were barefoot despite the cold. Silk wore a green dress that came down to her knees, fraying at the hem. The sleeves ended above her wrist, leaving her hands clear and free.

Vita felt by candlelight for her clothes. She pulled on her grandma's liquid-soft silk shirt, and her bright red skirt, falling full to the knee, perfect for running. She retied the laces on her boots. From her own bag she took a square of oil cloth and shoved it in her back pocket, added a stub of candle, then double-checked her penknife. She flicked it open and tested the edge of the blade with her thumb. It was sharp.

Her hands were shaking. 'Ready?' She turned her collar up, and smelt the dry sweetness of her grandmother's perfume.

'Let's go treasure-hunting,' said Arkady.

They waited while Silk knelt at the door, her lock-pick in hand.

'What were you going to do if we *had* run off? How were you going to get out?' she asked Vita.

'I've been learning,' said Vita. She pulled out a

length of wire from her pocket and showed Silk. 'I reckoned it might take me an hour or two, but I'd get there in the end.'

A smile twitched – unwillingly, fleetingly – at Silk's lip. 'Well,' she said, and the lock clicked under her hand, 'that didn't take an hour.'

Vita peered under the door, looking for feet, or any trace of a guard. 'They should both be outside. I think they'll be digging.' Adrenaline was starting to fizz through her blood, and she felt her whole body quickening.

She pushed open the door. The corridor was lit by a single gas lamp on the wall.

'Nobody,' she said, and the four children edged into the hall.

'Which way?' whispered Samuel.

'Grandpa said it's in the old hiding place. That almost certainly means the safe. The safe is in the drawing room,' said Vita. 'This way.'

'But if it's there, in the safe, won't Sorrotore have already found it?' asked Silk.

Vita shook her head. 'It's not an obvious safe. It's

not behind one of the paintings, or anything like that. It's hidden.'

They tiptoed down the passageway, and came out in the kitchen, then passed through a swinging door into the entrance hall.

The hall was as huge as it was dirty, but the moonlight cast the blue walls into navy. The flagstoned floor was cold even through her shoes, and the vast crystal chandelier still hung from a rope of chains above, dusty and candle-less.

She leaned against the old grandfather clock, closed her eyes, and summoned up the blueprint in her mind. She could see it clearly – every room, labelled in neat block capitals.

'The drawing room is through here,' she said. A marble-paved corridor led off the hall. 'Second door to the left.' They darted in, and Vita closed the door soundlessly behind them.

Four pent-up breaths were released, and then, as Vita's torchlight cast across the room, Arkady gasped. Most of the furniture had been sold by Grandpa and Grandma, but the few sofas and armchairs which remained had been torn open in the back and seat, and the stuffing lay in piles on the floor of the room. The stuffed polar bear head lay cut open on the floor.

'He's been searching,' said Arkady.

'Someone should guard the door,' said Vita.

Silk nodded. 'I'll watch through the keyhole.'

'Where's the safe?' asked Samuel.

Vita gestured at the vast fireplace. 'In there.'

'Under the floor?'

'No. It's inside the chimney. Grandpa said it meant you got covered in soot every time you opened it, but it'd never be found.'

Vita crossed to the fireplace. It was as large as a wardrobe, and the chimney was vast, wide enough to fit a filing cabinet inside. 'I can't see ... Wait, no, I can! I see it – but it's at least halfway up the chimney!'

'Do you know the code?' asked Samuel.

Vita nodded. 'It's my birthday.'

Samuel came to join her, and looked up the chimney. 'Do you want me to go?' he said quietly.

249

Her foot was screaming yes, but Vita shook her head. This was the final stage: it had to be her. 'I've got to do it.'

She rubbed at her left leg, to put the life back into it, and ducked into the chimney. She lifted her left shoe and set it against the opposite wall. She braced herself, then lifted the other leg, pressing her back against the wall. Slowly, painfully, she began to wriggle upwards, her knees shaking with the effort.

'*Good!*' Arkady whispered.

Her head was inside the chimney; then her torso and shoulders. She breathed in, and soot pressed against the back of her throat.

Then a sound, so quiet it could be the breath of the house, made Vita freeze.

It was Silk's voice. 'Someone's coming!'

Frantically Vita clicked off her torch and edged herself higher, dragging the skin of her back against the wall, until the whole of her body was wedged inside the chimney. She could see nothing except blackness. There was a barely audible scuffling as the others dived for hiding places.

And then the door opened.

Vita, peering down past her own body at the floor, saw the room illuminate with torchlight, followed by slow footsteps.

She squeezed her eyes shut. It was like an agonising, hideous game of hide-and-seek.

The footsteps came further into the room. Vita's spine was aching, and the dust in her throat was starting to sting. She fought back the urge to cough.

The feet sounded as though they were retreating. The light moved towards the door; then it hesitated, and flicked once more around the room. There was a thud; it sounded as though the guard had kicked a sofa. Dust billowed suddenly up the chimney, and Vita's body convulsed as she let out the smallest sound – a strangulated, muted cough.

The feet paused. Then another man's voice came down the corridor, too faint to hear, but the impatience in it was clear. The man in the room grunted. Feet strode out, closing the door behind them.

There was silence. Then, in the quietest of whispers, Samuel spoke. His voice was near the chimney.

'Are you all right in there?'

'Yes,' said Vita. 'Who was it?'

'The guard,' said Silk.

'You said they'd be digging,' said Arkady.

'I thought they would be,' said Vita.

She tensed every muscle, and gritted every single tooth, and pushed herself the last six inches higher into the chimney. It was narrower now. In the wall to the left of her, at the height of her shoulder, she felt the sudden chill of iron.

She switched on the torch.

She could see her knuckles, skinned and stained with something dark and wet. She could also see, set into the door of the safe, a dial. Slowly, her arms cramped and hands fumbling inside the chimney, she turned it.

The door clicked. It was almost impossible to open, in the small space, with her own head and shoulders in the way. She peered in.

There was nothing. No box, no green gleam of an emerald.

Cold misery swooped over her. She edged a hand in, keeping the other braced against the wall.

Her hand met a handful of papers – some full sheets, some scraps. She dragged them out, and stuffed them, for want of a better place, down her front. Then she wriggled downwards, until the dark ground was close enough to drop. She landed, painfully, on top of her own leg, and stood. It was a struggle not to cry: not from the pain, but from the doubt that had swept over her.

The other three stood clustered around the mantelpiece in complete darkness.

'Anything?' whispered Silk.

Vita gave a tiny shake of her head. 'This is all there was,' she said. She fished out the papers from her top, folded them tightly into a block of paper the size of her palm, and stuffed them into the waistband of her skirt.

There was a pause, in which Vita tried to haul her heart up from the floor.

'Don't look like that,' said Samuel. 'Is there anywhere else it could be?'

'Presumably,' said Silk, 'it could be anywhere in the entire house.' Her voice was tight with nerves. 'Which – I don't know if you noticed – is a large one.'

'Did your grandpa ever talk about other hiding places?' said Arkady. 'Do you have a Plan B?'

Slowly Vita nodded. She had hoped so hard that she wouldn't have to use it.

Arkady brightened. 'I knew you would! Where? Tell!'

'There's a place my grandpa discovered when he was just a kid – but I was so sure it would be in the safe!'

'Where is it? Tell!'

Vita swallowed. 'In the turret.'

'The same turret that you said is about to collapse?' said Silk.

'That one,' said Vita. 'Let's go.'

They went single file down the corridor, glancing over their shoulders, until they reached the end of the hallway. It widened to another sweeping stair-case, broad enough for them to run up four abreast. It had once been polished, and it still gleamed a glorious rich oak, but it was pockmarked with woodworm and damp. One side was lit by the moon.

Vita led the way, keeping to the shadowy side, where the stars could not reach them. Her muscles were so tense she could feel them contracting under her skin.

At the top of the stairs, there was a hallway, exactly as she had known it would be, waiting for her as if she had been there a dozen times before. She remembered everything she had taught herself, and the relief of it was like a gasp of oxygen in the night.

Vita turned left. As they crept along the corridor, a wooden plank creaked under Arkady's foot, as loud, it seemed to Vita, as a scream, and they all froze.

The house fell silent. It settled back into its dust and majesty.

'It's OK,' said Vita.

Suddenly a noise like a cannon shot rang out. Silk, Samuel and Arkady flattened themselves against the wall, but Vita ran to the window. Only one thing could be that loud, here, in the middle of nowhere: the sound of a huge chunk of wood slamming into place. Outside the front door was the jetty, and moored at the jetty was a small boat, its chrome edging glinting in the moonlight.

'The front door,' Vita breathed. Her hand went to her penknife. 'He's here.'

CHAPTER TWENTY-TWO

For a moment, Vita was obliterated. Instinct seized her and shook her like a rat; it told her to push the others out of the way, tear down the stairs, leap into the water and swim home.

Get out, said her blood. *Leave the others. Go.*

She gripped the window sill and waited for it to pass. It did, as it had always done before, and left her feeling sick to her stomach. It had felt like a sharp hour, but it had only been seconds: the others were still standing in the corridor, waiting for her to tell them what to do.

She turned to them, lifted her chin and pushed back her shoulders so she faced the night like a detective, like a cat, like an acrobat.

'He'll either go and check on us straight away, or he'll go to the garden and see if they've found the jewel. I think that's more likely.'

'Yes,' said Silk.

'Either way, he'll soon find out we've escaped,' said Vita. 'And he'll start searching the house.' She spoke so quickly her words collided, and the others leaned closer. 'Listen. This place has twenty-six rooms. If he searches each of them properly, and starts from the bottom floor, it *could* take him twenty-six minutes to reach the last one.'

'No. A minute's a long time. More like thirty seconds per room – so, thirteen,' said Arkady, but his eyes were beginning to shine again, as he understood what she meant.

'The way out,' said Vita. She spoke quickly. 'You need to know where it is. There's a grate in the wall, in the back of the cellar – it's just a gap with a grating over it – it's where the waste pipe used to be.'

'*Waste pipe?* That's your escape route? A drain?'

'Not any more – now it's just a grate. It's bolted to the wall, but it unscrews from the inside. Silk should be able to use a lock-pick on it. It drops straight into the lake – that's why it's exit-only – so you'll have to swim.' She stepped backwards, down the corridor, away from them.

'He's here. I'm so sorry – this wasn't how I thought it would be. You need to go.'

Arkady gave a snort that sounded like a laugh. 'We're not leaving you here!'

'Yes you are! We didn't know Sorrotore would come – I would never have brought you here—'

'What are you planning?' said Samuel.

'I'm going to the turret. That's the last place he'll look. It was boarded up years ago, when it got too dangerous. He might not even come up there. Maybe.'

'But what if you get trapped?' said Silk. Her voice was very quiet. 'Vita, maybe you're right – maybe we should leave. But if we're going, you have to come with us. This isn't a game; you don't know what he might do if he finds you.'

Vita shook her head. 'I swore.'

'Your grandfather wouldn't want you to do this!' said Silk.

'I *swore*.' As urgent as the fear was the image of Grandpa – how he would take the emerald in his twisted fingers, holding it up so the light would catch its glow, and the smile that would break across his face. 'I know it's not a game! When I find that necklace, *everything* changes.'

'Well, we've already wasted a full minute,' said Samuel. 'Go.'

'I'm coming,' said Silk. 'If you're going to be stupid, I might as well be too. There might be locks.'

'Ark and I will keep watch on the floor below,' said Samuel, 'and send a signal if he comes up.'

Vita nodded. She wanted to find words that were large enough for the ache in her chest – words that were more than ordinary, day-to-day language – but there was no time, and Sorrotore might be anywhere.

So she only said, 'Thank you,' and ran.

CHAPTER TWENTY-THREE

Vita left her torch with the boys. She led the way down the dark corridor, one hand running along the stone wall, until she reached another staircase. She limped up it, Silk following, breathing hard. The staircase led to a landing, and more rooms, stretching left and right.

'Left,' she whispered.

The door at the end of the corridor was smaller than the others. It was padlocked closed.

'All right,' said Silk. Her face was lined, her

eyebrows almost touching in the middle. She knelt, and slid her lock-pick into the padlock. She fiddled with it. A frown came over her face.

'Who fitted this?'

'Grandpa. It leads to the tower. He didn't want anyone getting up there.'

'It's odd … It's been chewed.'

'Chewed? By an animal?'

Silk shook her head. 'The mechanism's off – like the last time someone locked it, they attacked the inside with a screwdriver. Like someone wanted to make sure nobody ever opened it again.'

Vita's heart fell. 'So what does that mean? We can't get in?'

'No,' said Silk. She swapped the lock-pick for a longer, thinner hook from her stocking top. 'It's just going to take longer.'

'We don't have longer!'

Silk glared at her. 'I had picked up on that,' she said. 'Do you have a light?'

Vita struck a match, and Silk was illuminated, her hands lightly resting on the lock, as if her fingertips could listen to its insides.

Far below, there was the sudden sound of a slamming door. Vita jerked the match and it went out, but
she said nothing.

Silk drew a deep breath, fitted a new shard of metal
into the lock, and did not exhale until the padlock
gave a small, barely audible click. She tore it off and
handed it to Vita, who shoved it in her pocket and
hauled back the door. It groaned on its hinges.

Behind the door was a spiral staircase, made of
uneven slabs of stone, worn smooth as marble by feet
and time. A cobweb hung down from the curved
ceiling, turning from grey to silver in the light of the
match Vita struck.

'If you don't want to come,' Vita said, 'I would
completely understand.'

Silk snorted. She did not bother to reply.

Vita started up the stairs, as fast as she could force
her body to go. Silk followed, pulling the door shut
behind her.

The dark here was absolute, and Vita paused on
the stairs to strike another match, fumbling for the

emergency candle stub in her pocket. If ever there was an emergency, she told herself, this was it.

'How high is it?' breathed Silk.

'It can't be much further,' said Vita. As she spoke, the staircase widened to a tower room, barely ten feet across each way but vastly high. In one corner was a steep wooden staircase, leading to a door set thirty feet high in the wall, so small it was almost a window.

'Up there?'

Together they took in the staircase. It looked half ruined; as if something had waged war on it over the years, with teeth and claws and small weaponry.

'Woodworm,' said Vita.

'Is it safe?' asked Silk.

'I think I've seen safer things,' said Vita. 'But that's the only way.'

'What's at the top?'

'The sky,' said Vita. 'I'll go first.'

She put one foot in the middle of the first step, and felt the wood dip. She took a second step, a third, and the staircase cracked like fire. Something under her foot snapped. She moved faster, on hands and knees, feeling the wood give under her palms. Silk followed; her foot went straight through one step, and she hissed but did not cry out. Vita was near the top when a sound below – far below, on the stone steps – made her freeze.

Someone was coming up to the tower.

Vita took the last steps at a run, reached the small wooden door, shoved it open and darted through. She found herself standing on the stone floor of a circular tower, open to the sky. Silk followed, shutting the door soundlessly behind her. They peered under the gap of the door, back down the wooden stairs into the dark.

The flickering light of a gas lamp drenched the small room below them. A head appeared, then a broad-shouldered body.

Sorrotore paused, breathing in dust, staring up at the staircase. The wood looked, from Vita's vantage point, shipwrecked. He grunted, and crossed to it.

The first step he took caused the stair to splinter. He grimaced, and was just taking the second step when there was a noise – it wasn't a door slamming, or the wind. It was a yell of triumph, a *whoop!* that echoed and rebounded against the walls.

'Vita!' A shout came filtering through the building. 'I've found it!'

'Arkady,' breathed Vita.

Sorrotore froze. Then he turned and hurled himself back the way he had come.

'He's found it!' whispered Silk. 'Let's go! The cellar!'

'Wait!' said Vita.

'Why? Come *on*! Arkady found the necklace!'

'But he wouldn't yell if he found it! He's not an idiot.'

Silk snorted.

'He's *not*,' said Vita. 'He's smart – properly smart. There's something wrong.'

'But he sounded happy!'

'What if he was trying to get Sorrotore back down the stairs? What if Arkady knew we'd been cornered?'

Silk caught her meaning. 'What now?'

Vita's mind spun. 'We go back down – but quietly.

266

Take some of the wood from the stairs as a weapon. Try to get him from behind.'

'But if Arkady and Samuel *haven't* found it down there, then it's up here, and if it's up here, we're not leaving till we have it.'

'I'm not staying up here if he's got Arkady and Samuel.' Vita tried to move past Silk. 'It's my fault they're here—'

'No!' Silk pushed Vita back. 'They would kill us if we gave up now. Where's the hiding place?'

Vita shook herself. 'It's – I don't know. It's a loose stone in the tallest tower.'

Silk looked, dismayed, at the stones around them. 'You're joking. Nothing to narrow that down?'

'No.' The word felt heavy in Vita's mouth.

'Think, Vita!'

With an immense effort, Vita hauled her mind back – out from her feet, out from her stomach, out from her panicking, roaring chest. 'He was a jeweller,' she said. 'He said almost anything can be a jewel. Look for beautiful stones.'

'They're not beautiful! They're stones!'

But, in the merging of candlelight and moonlight, some *were* more beautiful than others. Some were stern grey, but others were streaked with purple, spotted with blue, veined with white.

Vita scanned the walls, reaching out to push and pull at the stones that were speckled, or shaped like continents. Silk crouched low over the base-level stones, muttering, 'Beautiful stones. Sure. Luxury rocks. Why not?' under her breath.

The tower was circular, and barely five paces in diameter, but it stretched high above Vita's head. She was just beginning to wonder what she would do if it was one of the high-set stones when she felt a sudden give under her fingers.

She looked again at the stone under her palm. It was an almost perfect square, grey, with a ragged, bluish lightning bolt running through it.

She dug her fingers into the mortar around the edge of the rock and pulled. The stone screeched, stone against mortar against nails, but it came, slowly at first, and then suddenly it was in her arms and she had dropped it on the flagstoned floor of the tower, almost crushing her own foot.

'Silk!' Vita's voice was jagged with sudden, inexplicable tears. 'Silk!'

Silk turned, and her eyes and mouth fell open. There, in the candlelight, wedged on its side in the heart of the wall, was a wooden box.

'It's here,' whispered Vita.

Silk's voice sounded husky, knocked sideways with it. 'I didn't believe it! I can't believe it!'

Vita's hands shook as she reached in and pulled the box out. Her fingers got pinched and the skin grazed off two fingertips, but she didn't feel it.

The box was dusty and covered in bits of mortar. It was as wide and long as a child's outspread hand. She wiped it with her sleeve, and the rich brown wood shone through. She shook it; there was no rattle of jewels, but there was the muffled thud of something wrapped in cloth. She dug her nail under the lid and tried to open it.

She tried again, harder. 'It doesn't open!' Vita stared at the box, turned it over in her hands. 'There's no lock.'

Silk took it. 'There'll be a concealed lock some-where. Can I—'

But as she spoke, there was a scream from down-stairs. Vita's eyes met Silk's.

'Samuel! Let's go.' Vita pulled the oil cloth from her back pocket and fumbled to wrap the box in it as she limped. She shoved the box down the front of her shirt, cold against her skin.

Vita tried to take the stairs at a sprint. All the years of being told to *slow down, take care* were, just for that second, pushed away, and she ran, her boots thumping, down the steps towards Samuel and Arkady. Once Silk slipped and landed with a crack on her hip and swore, but was up again and pushing Vita in the back when she turned to offer help.

They burst out of the wooden door into the corridor, no longer wary of the noise.

'Wait!' panted Silk. 'We need to listen.'

Vita tried to hold her breath. The house was utterly silent. Then it came again: a scream that rose and rose again before it fell.

Vita frowned. It wasn't a scream of panic – it was deliberate, a shriek that cut through the icy air like a battle cry.

'It's coming from downstairs,' said Silk.

'Let's go,' said Vita.

They moved as quietly as they could down the dark corridor, passing silent closed doors.

One of the doors flew open and a figure burst out of it. It tackled Vita round the middle, pinning her hands to her sides, and drove her, nose first, to the ground.

She fought one arm free and was about to claw at the face when a voice gasped, 'Vita!' and the grip let go. 'I thought it was Sorrotore!'

It was Arkady. He rolled sideways and jumped to his feet. 'Are you OK?'

She was not – some nerve deep in the bridge of her foot had caught fire – but she only said, 'What happened? Tell!'

'I saw Sorrotore going past, the way you had gone, so I ran to the bedroom opposite, and shouted that I had the jewels – and he came charging in. I hid inside the chest of drawers – I thought the wardrobe would be too obvious – and he was just about to open them, and then …'

'And then?' said Vita.

'Samuel screamed. But not from the bedroom. From somewhere downstairs. And Sorrotore made this noise – like a cat spitting – and ran. But I saw through a crack in the wood – Vita, he has a gun.'

'Come on,' said Vita. She got slowly to her feet and tried out her left leg. It held. 'Samuel!'

'Do we go quietly, or charge?' said Silk.

'Quietly,' said Vita. 'For now. We need to see what's happening.'

Arkady handed Vita the torch and she led the way to the top of the staircase. She paused. 'Something's going on.'

No further screams came, but fast footsteps rang on the marble floor of the hall.

Then a voice bellowed, 'Boy! There's no way out, boy! Where are you? This isn't a game.'

Vita led the way down the staircase, taking care to

step at the far edge, where the woodworm was least thorough and the staircase creaked less.

At the bend in the hallway, she hesitated. If they went a step further, Sorrotore would see them.

Vita looked at Arkady, who looked at Silk, who looked at Vita.

'That's my best friend in there,' said Arkady. 'I'm not being quiet.'

'Then let's charge,' said Vita.

Arkady let out a great war cry and they ran, legs flying, Vita leading, down the last feet of the corridor and into the great stone hall. Sorrotore stood in the centre of the cavernous space, a lamp in one hand, a shotgun in the other. He whipped round.

At that moment, several things happened. Sorrotore saw Vita. He let out a shout – a sound that was so choked with rage that Vita stopped where she stood, frozen, staring, not breathing. She had never seen anger laid out so raw on the skin; she had never seen a face more frightening.

At the same moment, from the highest window,

forty feet up, a figure came swinging down on a rope. The rope was tied to the bars in the window, and it creaked and strained as the body soared through the air.

Everyone looked up. Mid-air, Samuel let go of the rope, snatched the bottom of the chandelier, and swayed above them, the larger crystal drops crashing together, the smaller ones falling to earth like hail.

Sorrotore stood staring, incredulous, at the sight.

'Run!' Vita whispered to Silk and Arkady. 'Get to the cellar. Start taking the grate off.' They hesitated, and she pushed them. 'Please!'

And this time they ran, tearing past Sorrotore, whose face was trained on the boy pulling himself up the structure of the chandelier to cling to the chain from which it hung.

Vita ran with them, a few paces behind, but swerved at the edge of the hall to crouch behind the grandfather clock, its broken face pointing to midnight.

'Boy! Was it you who shouted? Do you have the emerald?' said Sorrotore.

Samuel said nothing.

Vita's hand was at her penknife. She flicked open the blade. She calculated, with the precision of a professional, the exact curve the knife would have to fly to dig into Sorrotore's chest.

But she could not let it go. She thought of her grandfather, and his easy trust in her. *'Your weapon in life is not going to be a knife.'* Her wrist would not bend and flick and release. Her body was rigid.

'Get down right now, boy,' said Sorrotore, 'or I will shoot you first, and then your friends.'

To throw the knife would be death. Vita's body began to shake where she crouched, hidden, watching. She wanted nothing to do with death – nothing to do with finality, with endings, with the dark of it. She hated the man more than she hated any living thing, but he was living.

Samuel's eyes were wide and staring.

Throw the knife, Vita screamed inwardly. *Throw it.*

Her knife hand fell to her side, and as it did she felt, in her pocket, the heft of the rusted padlock from the tower.

She pulled it out, and her body was suddenly her own again. She took aim – a brief, sharp calculation of distance and angle – her arm drew back at the shoulder, and she threw.

The lock struck Sorrotore on the temple, just above his left ear. He staggered backwards, one step, a second step, and then crumpled like a puppet with its strings cut.

Vita scrambled to her feet. 'Samuel! Can you jump down?'

Samuel looked down at the stone floor. He shook his head. 'Not on to stone. I'll shatter my ankle.'

'Don't move! I'll find a ladder,' she called, and though she felt so stiff she could barely stand, she made to run down the corridor.

'Hang on!' Samuel shook his head, high above her. He began to pump his body back and forth, so that the chandelier swung crazily on its chain, shedding crystals on to Sorrotore's body below. At the furthest swing, he made as if to let go – but he hesitated, his face lined with fear, and swung back.

Vita remembered; remembered the vivid joy with which he had soared in the midnight ballroom, remembered the words he had used.

'*Listo!*' she called. 'Samuel, *listo!*'

His voice was a gasp. 'Ready!'

The chandelier swung up, up to the right, and, '*Hep!*' yelled Vita, and with a cry that echoed round the great hall, he let go of the clattering chandelier and soared through the air.

He flew past Vita, stretched out his arms, spun once, twice, in a double somersault, and hit the soft, worm-eaten wood of the corridor, landing on his shoulder and rolling twice, jumping up and rubbing his side and grimacing.

'Are you hurt?' she asked him. She crossed to Sorrotore, snatched up his gun, and ran to Samuel. The wood had scraped at his skin. 'You're bleeding!'

He didn't bother to answer. 'Did you get it?'

It took Vita half a second to remember what he meant.

'Yes,' she said. There was no triumph in it now. She looked at the mess of shattered crystals, at the man lying among them. She spoke the words of all heroes, criminals, and escape artists.

'Let's get out of here.'

CHAPTER TWENTY-FOUR

They ran, looking back over their shoulders every step. As they limped through the kitchen they heard, very faintly, the sounds of the guard and his companion, the clang of metal spades. They reached the cellar to find it empty. Vita cast her fading torch around the room. The stuffy smell of dust had gone, and the cold night wind blew in through an open hole cut straight into the wall, perhaps a foot across. They peered out. On the other side there was no bank, no earth: just a direct short drop into the lake.

Vita dropped Sorrotore's gun out of the hole, then looked at the width of Samuel's shoulders, and felt a sudden terror. 'Will you fit?'

'Only one way to find out,' he said. 'You go first.'

'No!' said Vita, 'You're bigger, so you first. If I fit and you don't, you'll be stuck here alone.'

He looked as if he were about to argue, but she pushed him towards the hole.

'Don't be so noble! It's just logic!'

'Fine,' he said. He went feet first, arms over his head to make his shoulders as narrow as he could. His skin, already raw from his landing, scraped against the stone. He said nothing, only pushed himself backwards, his eyes screwed up with pain.

'I'm stuck!' he gasped.

As he spoke, the door above them began to open.

Vita dropped the torch, put both her hands on his arms and gave him a great shove. There was a gasp as he fell, and then a splash, and she darted away from the dying torch, into the darkness, down one of the rows of shelves, and ducked low behind some bottles of red wine.

Sorrotore's polished black shoes came through the door, down the stairs, and paused, his eyes taking in the open grate and the spinning torch. It flickered and went out.

'I know you're still here,' he called, and his voice echoed through the darkness. 'I can hear you breathing.'

His footsteps rang down the corridors of wine bottles. He carried a small oil lamp; the light was two rows away from her. Vita tried to shuffle backwards and found she could not move.

'Enough, child,' came the voice. It was cold as the stone floor. 'I've had enough.'

In the blackness, Vita crouched. Her fear welled up in her, and for once she could not beat it down. It threatened to cover her head. It rose, and as it rose her body became frozen, animal, something foreign clothed in her own skin.

And she thought: *I can't.*

And she thought, unbidden, of the elephant, chained on the stage. Its hopelessness was her hopelessness.

And the fear rose over her head, and she was covered in it.

And her beating heart summoned up the elephant again, chained, and with it came the memory it had first conjured, of Jack Welles, her grandpa: her grandpa as he had been, drawing bullseyes on hospital walls, so unruly and so talented, and so alive.

And the fear crossed paths with the love, and the two merged.

And the love became her weapon.

And she rose with a shout of the kind of fury that Sorrotore had never dreamed, and flew at him.

This was nothing like the fight in the alley with a gang of pickpockets. This was rage, on both parts; his rage at this sudden prospect of failure, at this staring, ugly, maimed child; her rage at the stupidity of a world that admired men who took so much and broke so much.

He was larger but she was angrier, and she, despite her age and size, was the more ruthless of the two, and the more accustomed to pain. His hand grasped her round the middle, and she twisted and bit down

282

on skin, she was not sure what or where, but hard enough to draw blood. He shook her like an animal; like an animal fighting an animal.

Her hand swept backwards, found the neck of a bottle, gripped it, and swung it at his head. And he was down, for a second, slipping in the spilt alcohol and glass, and she ran for the open grate.

He was up again, wet, gasping, and he made a start towards her.

Vita flicked open the blade of her penknife, breathed a single breath in which she took aim, and threw. It went straight and true through the heart of the glass whisky bottle behind his head. The bottle exploded, coating Sorrotore's hair with whisky and knocking the other dozen bottles to the floor. Glass flew everywhere, rebounding off the walls. With a roar, Sorrotore ducked, putting up his hand to protect his eyes.

Vita darted to the hole in the wall. She laid a hand on the brick, steadied herself, turned.

'Your man, Dillinger,' said Vita. 'He said I was playing with fire.'

283

And she focused all of her anger and fear down into her hand. She snatched up her torch, spun it in her fingertips, and threw it, not at the bottles, but at the oil lamp Sorrotore had placed on the floor. It exploded; the flames caught at the whisky, snaking across the ground towards Sorrotore.

She gasped, and took in a mouthful of smoke, as the flames reached Sorrotore's oiled, profoundly flammable hair. He screamed, trying to smother them with his jacket.

She pushed herself through the thick wall, and fell head first through the air. The water was hard as earth as she hit it, but it opened to receive her, and she was tumbling, over and over, through the dark water.

It was pitch black. No way was up. She forced herself not to panic. She opened her eyes and spun, disorientated. Then she remembered: you breathe out bubbles – they rise to the surface. She blurted out half the air in her chest, inhaling some water in return, trying not to choke – and the bubbles rose, sideways it seemed to her, but she swam after them, one hand clutched to the box under her shirt, one straining at the water.

Her head broke free and she gasped, spitting and choking, for mouthful after mouthful of air. Ahead of her in the moonlight, a figure was just emerging from the lake at the shore: Samuel. Hands reached out to pull him into the bushes.

She struck out wildly, thrashing in the water, then remembered the watching eyes. '*Careful!*' she whispered to herself, and tried to swim under the surface, her chest red hot with water and smoke, her arms and legs forcing the water behind her with a strength that was more desperation than muscle. Every second she expected to hear the motorboat coming after her. She risked a glance. Smoke was snaking from the gap in the castle wall.

She kicked again and felt her feet hit earth. She stood up in the mud, fell to her knees, stood again, and stumbled into the hands of Silk, who had waded waist-deep to grab her wrist, and now pulled her into the bushes.

Arkady and Samuel were waiting, soaking wet.

With them were the dogs, Viking and Hunter, also soaking wet.

'I think they escaped down the jetty when all the men were coming in to dig,' said Arkady. 'I'm taking them with us.'

Without another word they stumbled together, Vita's leg shrieking in pain, mud-covered and soaking, through the night to reach the horses. They whinnied in recognition at Arkady's face and he climbed on to one, and hauled Vita, who was fighting to stay vertical, up in front.

Silk held out her hand, cupped, and Samuel stepped into it. Blood dripped from a deep graze on his shoulder on to the bay mare, but he reached out with his good hand and helped Silk swing up behind him. They went at a gallop, through the wood, Viking and Hunter loping on either side of Arkady's horse, out on to the country roads, clinging on to each other, riding straight into the sunrise.

As they went, it began to snow.

Back at the castle, the guard looked up from the

eight-foot-deep hole in which he stood, and sniffed, then went running. He discovered a half-doused fire, a barely conscious Sorrotore lying on the stairs, and a great deal of broken glass. He roared for buckets, for water, for help.

And in a corner, where the fire had not yet reached, was a pile of clothes, belonging to the kind of children who had never had a dangerous thought in their lives.

CHAPTER TWENTY-FIVE

The next train wasn't for several hours. The black horse lay down on the platform, and the four humans and two dogs curled up against it, seeking each other's soft animal heat. Arkady found some horse blankets in the field, but even so, by the time they scrambled on to the train, every inch of Vita ached. She clenched her jaw shut to stop her teeth from chattering.

The train was blessedly warm, though, and soon their clothes were steaming, misting the windows of their carriage on the inside. A food cart passed through the train. Arkady found a dime in his pocket, and they shared a single hot chocolate between four, drinking without waiting for it to cool. Then Vita tucked her feet up under her, ignoring the rule she'd been taught about no-shoes-on-seats, and leaned against the corner of the carriage.

She woke as they approached New York. Silk and Arkady were asleep, but Samuel was still staring out of the window. He turned to Vita.

'I've been trying to work it out – that red book. It didn't just have the plan in it – not just the map and the train times and all that. In the back, I saw there was … like a diary. About your grandfather, and the knife. What was that for?'

'That was for Sorrotore too,' said Vita. 'I wanted him to know what kind of man he had tried to hurt.'

At Grand Central Station the ceiling stars winked in welcome. They trudged, shivering, through the snow, the two German Shepherds following, across West 45th and up Seventh Avenue, out of Times

Square and towards Carnegie Hall.

'I wonder if they've noticed we're gone at home,' said Arkady.

'I think it's safe to assume,' said Samuel, 'that they have.'

'I wonder what they'll do to us.'

Vita was wondering the same thing; she tried to silence the thought. The trouble that she would be in on her return had seemed so insignificant compared to the danger of going that she had barely considered it. Now the thought was proving itself to be more than usually loud.

They turned the corner, and Vita's heart dropped. A cluster of people stood on the pavement outside Carnegie Hall: Arkady's mother and father; Morgan Kawadza, his face tight with fury; and Maiko the acrobat. A policeman was taking notes. At the edge of the group stood her mother, scanning the street. Her eyes were desperate.

Silk darted back around the corner. The others followed.

'I'm not coming!' she said. 'I'll go on to the Bowery.'

'No!' said Arkady. 'The police won't recognise you – it's not the same man. And we have to stick together. Anyway, don't you want to see the emerald?'

They came round the corner together: lake-stained, travel-stained, exhausted. There was a heartbeat pause – and then a fox-like call rang through the air, and Julia Marlowe came sprinting up the street.

She lifted Vita clean off the ground, pulling her against her chest as if she would bond them into one.

'Where have you been? Are you hurt? You're bleeding! What happened? *What have you done?*'

Vita buried her face in her mother's shoulder, and smelt her perfume. She wrapped her arms around her mother's neck. Even when her mother loosened her grip to wipe her eyes, Vita did not let go.

The policeman left, muttering under his breath, and for a few moments there was just-barely-restrained chaos. Arkady was simultaneously cuffed and embraced by his mother, while his father stood by, ramrod with fury. Samuel stood utterly still in front of his uncle, who spoke at him in a low voice in Shona, his whole body shaking with emotion. Silk stood apart, her eyes on the ground.

'We should go inside, into the warmth.' Mr Lazarenko spoke with a strong Russian accent, and his voice was full of barely controlled ire. 'You all better have a very good excuse for the night you just put us through.'

They crossed into the great marble hall. The two dogs followed Arkady.

'Come to the main stage,' said Mrs Lazarenko. 'They'll already be heating it for the matinee. And there's someone waiting.'

They filed in. The German Shepherds climbed on to two of the velvet seats and fell asleep. Vita, though, saw nothing but the figure sitting on a wooden chair in the centre of the stage. A voice rang through the great hall.

'Rapscallion. An explanation, please.'

Vita's grandfather rose to his feet. He stood, leaning on his stick, looking down at her. His face was cross-hatched with anger. He did not smile.

Vita's mother pushed her forwards. 'Go to him. He's been so afraid for you, and so angry. I thought he might have a heart attack.'

It is so rarely we are given the opportunity to prove ourselves by laying treasure at the feet of those we love. The space seemed to grow as Vita crossed it; it felt like she had traversed several miles as she climbed the steps to the stage and stood in front of him.

She unbuttoned her outer shirt and reached into her undervest. She pulled out the parcel. She unwrapped the oilcloth, still damp to the touch. She lifted out the wooden box and put it in her grandfather's hand.

The old man began to shake.

Grandpa's eyes sought Vita's. 'Rapscallion – how have you done this? What have you done?'

'We couldn't unlock it,' whispered Vita. 'We couldn't find a lock – we wondered if it was welded shut. It was in the tower.'

'In Hudson Castle? You went to the Castle?' He stared from Vita to Samuel to Silk and Arkady, who had followed, and who now stood in a corner of the main stage.

'Yes. We thought ... it had to be the one. It is, isn't it?'

He turned the box over. For one terrible moment, Vita was afraid he would not recognise it – that it was the wrong one, that she'd fought her way across a foreign land to bring back a box of nothing.

But his fingers slid over the wood, seeking something. He pressed, and the base of the front of the box slipped outwards, revealing a keyhole no bigger than Vita's little fingernail.

He reached for his watch chain. 'I kept the key strung here,' he said. 'I thought it was all I had left. I thought the box was gone. I thought the key was my all. I tried to tell myself it was enough.'

The key was miniature, and he fumbled with it in his arthritic hands. It clicked into the keyhole as if it had been last used only the hour before.

Vita thrust her hands into her pockets and crossed every finger she had.

Grandpa sat back down and set the box on his lap. His hands, which quivered daily, shook so hard it took him three tries to prise open the lid.

It opened with a creak of aged wood; the polish cracked along the top. Inside, untouched by the time it had spent in the lake, was a wadding of black velvet.

Grandpa had stopped breathing. He lifted one corner of the velvet, and his eyes welled with tears. His face, usually so white, flushed like a child's.

He pulled aside the velvet, and let out a soft cry of love and longing such as Vita had never heard before.

He lifted in his hands a single green pendant, as large as a lion's eye. His fingers fumbled at it, and found a clasp, and it sprang open on a hinge to reveal two photographs. One was of Grandpa, younger, but with the same long nose and broad brow.

Opposite him, in the other photograph, a woman looked out at the world with large and generous eyes. She was fine-boned, and her hair was turning grey at the temples. She smiled, and the smile was Vita's. And around her throat there was the emerald necklace.

Grandpa pressed his fingernail under the photograph, lifted it from the locket and brought it to his lips. The necklace slipped on to the floor, forgotten.

'Lizzy,' whispered her grandfather. Tears dropped down his face, catching and halting in the wrinkles in

295

his cheeks and nose. 'Oh, Lizzy. Oh my girl. My shining girl.'

Vita's mother rose to her feet.

'When she died,' said Grandpa, 'I put it in the tower and destroyed the lock. I vowed I'd never look at it again. I was so angry at her for leaving. For leaving me in the dead embers of the world. But you've returned her to me.'

Vita bent to pick up the necklace and put it in his lap.

He smiled at it. 'This old thing. Would you like it?' And he held it up to her, as if to set it on her neck.

'What do you mean?' A panic rose in Vita's heart. 'No! We have to sell it!'

'Sell it? What for?'

'That's how we're going to get a lawyer – we're going to sell it, and we're going to get Hudson Castle back. That's what all this was *for!*'

He understood and felt the pain of it at the same time. 'Oh, Rapscallion. It's not an emerald. It's coloured glass. Even the silver setting is plate.'

Vita's heart lurched. 'No! They were famous. The family jewels were famous!'

'They were, until they were all lost or sold. The emerald was the last to go. We sold it to pay for the roof.'

'But it looks—'

'So real? I know. I made a replica of the real thing, before we sent it off to the auction house. Lizzy loved it as much as if it was real. She'd put it on and say, "Buckle up your dancing shoes, Jack," and we'd go out and dine on the cheapest soups in the grandest restaurants. Ah, they were our glory days! But it's barely worth five dollars.'

The threat of tears caught in her throat. 'But,' she whispered, too low for him to hear, 'your home – I was going to get you back the Castle.'

Vita's whole body went suddenly limp, and she sat down with a thump on the floor. She had wanted so much. She had wanted to fight for him, and to win.

Try as she might, she could not stop a single tear running down her cheek.

But her grandfather was alight with happiness, and she tried to shake herself: he mustn't see her cry. She felt about for her handkerchief. She pulled out something from under her waistband, half dry, and was about to drag it across her nose when she halted. Two words at the top caught her eye: 'Hudson Castle'.

They were the papers from the safe, half drenched and delicate as tissue paper, but the printed ink had not run.

'I found these, too,' she said. Grandpa was still holding the photograph in both hands, so she passed them to her mother. 'Here, Mama – these were in the safe. In the chimney.'

Her mother stared at her, wide-eyed, her fury rushing back. 'In the *chimney safe*? Vita, what on this earth have you been—' But then her eye caught the printed lettering, and she stopped talking as suddenly as if she had been slapped. She took the papers with great care from Vita's hands and spread them out on the floor of the stage.

'What are they?' asked Vita.

'The title deeds to Hudson Castle,' said Vita's mother. 'Sorrotore didn't have them.' And her face flooded with sudden light. 'He never had them.'

*

It took some time for the riotous exclaiming to die down. Mama and Grandpa sat together, talking swiftly in whispers, his hands shaking with the shock and joy of it. The Lazarenkos and Morgan Kawadza still looked bewildered. There was still scepticism and anger in their eyes.

'We need the story from the beginning,' said Mrs Lazarenko.

'Now,' said Mr Lazarenko.

Samuel and Arkady looked at Vita. Silk looked at her hands.

'You tell it,' said Arkady. 'It's yours.'

'Begin with why,' said Mrs Lazarenko.

Vita found herself lost for words. It should be obvious, she thought. It was what you did: you fought for the people you love. She shook her head.

'Then begin with how,' said Morgan Kawadza. 'And what.'

Vita nodded. She looked only at Grandpa as she spoke, and that made it easier. His eyes alone shone like emeralds.

'It began, I guess, with the red book. It began with my plan.'

'That doesn't sound like the beginning, Rapscallion. The real beginning.'

So Vita went back – all the way back. Back to her great-great-great-grandfather, and his castle; back to Grandpa at her hospital bed, and on to Sorrotore and the lies that it had not occurred to anyone he would tell.

She described Silk's swift-fingered thieving, and Silk shook her head a quarter of an inch and stared fixedly at the wall, her face dark with embarrassment, or shame, or anger, or all three. Mr Lazarenko narrowed his eyes.

Vita described Arkady's mastery of birds and dogs and horses, and the way living things seemed to smell the hidden gentleness on his skin. She told them about finding Arkady riding Moscow through the streets, and Morgan Kawadza pulled his mouth tight at the corners.

She described Samuel's scramble up the wall of the Castle. She described the flight from the chandelier; the way he had cut through gravity as if it were optional, not for the likes of him. Samuel caught his uncle's eye, and he too ducked to face the wall.

'Swinging on the chandelier!' said Grandpa. 'What a thing, what a glorious thing!'

When at last she came to an end, there was a stunned silence.

Then Mr Lazarenko turned to Silk. 'You, girl.' He spoke brusquely. 'Show me what you can do. Show me if it's true.'

'Do you promise not to arrest me?' said Silk. 'It's illegal, what I do.'

Mr Lazarenko nodded, but his eyes were unbelieving and unimpressed.

Silk spoke softly. She turned to Julia. 'Would you have a coin that I might borrow?'

Julia fished in her pocket and handed over a dime.

'Would you,' said Silk, 'please go and sit in the front row? It's easier that way.'

The adults glanced at each other. Then Mr Lazarenko grunted, and they all filed past Silk, down on to the front row seats of the vast hall. Silk straightened her dress and combed the tail of her plait roughly with her fingers. The children followed the adults, and Silk stood alone, at the very edge of the stage.

Silk held up the dime. She clasped her hands together, then opened them, showing that the coin was gone. The adults politely applauded, but there was no great admiration in their eyes. Vita suppressed her grin. She bit her lip in anticipation.

Silk shrugged. 'It's just in my sleeve,' she said. 'You probably guessed.' She smiled shyly at Vita's mother. 'Mrs Marlowe, would you help me? Could you write something down for me?'

Vita's mother reached for the pen in her breast pocket, uncapped it. And then she stared at it, her whole body suddenly rigid.

'She's taken the ink cartridge out of my pen,' she said.

Silk smiled an almost invisible smile. 'Mr Lazarenko, if you look inside your right boot,' she said, 'there's a silk scarf that belongs to Vita's grandpa.'

Mr Lazarenko bent, staring at his boot, and pulled the bright red scarf out from his shoe. Grandpa stared down at his collar in shock.

'But – that's not possible—'

'Mr Marlowe,' said Silk softly, 'would you look in your left-hand pocket?'

Grandpa drew out a gold ring, and stared at it, open mouthed.

'That's mine!' said Morgan Kawadza. 'That's my signet ring!'

'O Bozhe,' breathed Mr Lazarenko. He turned to the children, and his face was transformed. He looked, suddenly, very much like Arkady. 'What else have you been hiding?'

The Gold Ballroom was empty when Arkady led his audience to it; empty, except for Moscow and Cork, who both came over to lick the boy in greeting. Arkady ignored Mr Lazarenko's startled exclamations about his dog, threw open the windows, leaned out, and whistled his sharp, longing whistle.

The birds descended like a thunderstorm; they came crowding in through every window, filling the air with feathers and clattering song.

Rasko looped around Arkady's head and came to rest on his shoulder. Rimsky came, croaking and laughing her throaty chuckle, from a nearby tree, and landed on Grandpa's arm. Grandpa gave a great shout of pleasure.

Arkady whistled again. Five minutes went by, and with every second more birds arrived. They flocked to him, crowding on to his shoulders; pigeons along one arm like a sleeve, a robin on his shoulder, a blue tit perched on the crown of his head.

Mr Lazarenko watched. 'What is this?'

Arkady grinned at his father, but the smile was uncertain at the edges. 'This is what I want. Not just the poodles, Papa – not just horses – I want everything. Dogs and horses and pigeons, and squirrels and rats and crows – all of the animals that people ignore, all dancing together – I want people to see them: *properly* see them. I want to make something completely new. It would be like being in the heart of the woods, in the middle of a theatre. Can you imagine?'

Mr Lazarenko's eyebrows had still not returned to their usual position on his face. Mrs Lazarenko, though, smiled, and in her smile there was pride enough to light a city.

'There is something here.' She spoke, not to the room, but to her husband. He met his wife's look with the understanding that comes from many years together.

She cocked her head in a question. Slowly, so slowly he seemed almost to be bowing, he nodded.

'What?' said Arkady.

'A troupe,' said Mr Lazarenko.

Morgan Kawadza raised his hand. 'Nikolai, no. Not Samuel.'

'Morgan. Hold judgement,' said Lazarenko, and he turned to Silk, who stood, one hand on Cork's enormous head. 'You. Girl. How would you feel about being asked to run away and join the circus?'

Silk stared at him, uncomprehending. 'What?'

'I'll find someone to train you. I can make you the greatest sleight-of-hand artiste on this continent. You could learn escape artistry – you can already pick a padlock. People will queue up to have their pockets picked by you.'

Silk's whole body seemed to sag and sway with shock. For the first time, Vita saw her lost for words.

'I … don't know. I'm not … I'm just not.' Silk turned, helpless, to the three other children, and their faces gave her courage. Silk drew breath, pushed her chin high. Already tall, she grew, in that moment, three more inches. 'Yes,' she said. 'I say yes.'

'To whom should I go – who is responsible for you? Your parents?' said Lazarenko.

Silk shook her head. 'I don't have a dad. My mother's dead a long time ago.'

'Any family at all?'

'There's no one,' said Silk. And she looked again at Arkady, at Samuel, at Vita, and there her eyes rested. 'There's never been anyone, until now.'

'A troupe, then,' said Lazarenko.

'There's prestige in a troupe, if you can make it fly,' said Maiko.

'An animal waltz,' said Mrs Lazarenko, 'a pick-pocket … and a knife-thrower.'

Vita had been struggling with the impression that she was in a dream. The exhaustion of the night before was pulling at her, and the horse trying to eat her hair did not help with the general sense of

306

unreality. But at this, her head snapped backwards, and she stared at Lazarenko.

'Me?'

'Yes,' said Mr Lazarenko. Already the shrewd business look was in his eyes. 'The circus can be a good home. It will take time. It's not easy. But you could be adequate, I think.'

Mrs Lazarenko gave a choke that was part laughter, part exasperation. 'Kolya! She's not a horse, to be haggled over. It sounds as though she could be more than adequate. It sounds as though she could be remarkable.'

'She is more than remarkable,' said Grandpa. 'She is an army unto herself.'

Vita looked at her mother and grandfather.

'Mama?' said Vita.

Her mother's look was complex. Dozens of expressions that Vita could not read played across her face, and a few that she could: pride, doubt, more than a dozen years' worth of protective fear. The look settled on love. 'Is it what you want?'

Vita looked around the stage; at the vast sweep and

scale of it. She thought of Lady Lavinia, of the ferocious elegance and precision in her hands and eyes. She thought of her twisted foot, of her thin calf and uneven shoes, and the thousands who would see it if she stood upon a stage every night.

She straightened her back, and set her chin like a boxer's.

'Is it yes?' said Lazarenko.

Vita felt her face split apart in a smile, and she was about to answer when Arkady scoffed.

'Of course yes! It was decided long ago. We're already a troupe.'

At the word 'troupe', Morgan Kawadza raised a hand. 'No!' he said. 'For the three of you, yes, if you wish. I'll help train your boy for you, Lazarenko, if he wants to know about horses – there might be talent there. But I know what you're thinking. And my answer's no: not Samuel. He is the heir to my act. And he's my responsibility; I swore to take care of him. I will not expose him to the carelessness and cruelty of the world.'

Samuel stood alone, his arms twisted and entwined.

'I want to fly,' he said. 'It's all I want. I know it won't be easy and I don't care, not even slightly.'

'It's impossible,' said Kawadza. 'So the boy can climb a wall and swing from a rope!'

But Vita was looking, not at Kawadza, but at Samuel, standing in the middle of the ballroom. The same clarity that she had seen on the trapeze was coming over his face.

'No,' said Samuel.

'*No* is not—' said Kawadza.

'OK! Fine! Then, *yes*,' said Samuel. '*Yes*, Uncle, I know you want to keep me safe. But it's not enough. And *yes*, I know it will be hard – harder than what's fair, harder than for anyone else – maybe so hard I fail.' And he untwisted his arms. 'But I'm going to fly anyway.'

And he took a run at the window, three storeys up.

'Stop!' shouted Kawadza.

But Samuel didn't stop. Samuel was not born to stop. His feet reached the window sill and he launched himself into the air. He dropped, pin-straight, and as he dropped he seized the flagpole that jutted out of the wall of Carnegie Hall. He spun around it like an Olympic gymnast, twice, three times. For one second he paused, his feet pointed to the sky. Then he let himself go again, twisted in the air, his arms crossed tight across his chest, and came to rest, right way up, on top of a parked car. He slid down to the pavement below.

He saluted.

Morgan Kawadza stared down at the New York City street – at the people bustling past each other, at the oblivious paperboy waving a newspaper, and at Samuel, standing shining and alone despite the stream of people, his head up to the sky.

Vita looked harder at the paper boy. She could just see the headline: the words 'BUSINESSMAN' and 'HUDSON' and 'INFERNO'.

A tear ran down Kawadza's cheeks. 'He flies,' he said. 'A boy who flies.'

CHAPTER TWENTY-SIX

The fire was investigated. Some things are impossible to brush under the carpet, and the story that soon spread, of a fire in a castle cellar and a gang of children with knives at their belts and wings on their feet, was one of them. Vita unpicked the signet ring from her skirt, and handed it to the investigators.

Sorrotore was in the hospital when he was arrested. The fire had been extinguished before it could spread to the rest of the castle. The skin on Sorrotore's scalp had suffered the worst of it, and his hair was almost entirely scorched off, leaving raw red skin behind.

A murder investigation was opened. Sorrotore's apartment was raided, and the paperwork discovered, along with a great deal of illegal bootleg liquor. Other fires connected with Sorrotore's properties were revisited, and a chain of fraudulent insurance claims and demolitions under eighteen different listed companies were discovered.

Dillinger was tracked down and arrested in a speakeasy. It was unclear whether he was sober enough to understand as he was read his rights, but, had anyone looked closely, they might have thought there was relief on his face.

'Playing with fire,' he said, and made a noise that may have been a laugh or may have been a choke.

'So Hudson Castle is back in your father's hands,' said Mr Lazarenko to Vita's mother. He had invited Vita and her mother to his dressing room in Carnegie Hall, 'to talk business'. Business talk was clearly something Lazarenko thrived upon; there was a sheen to him as he beckoned them in. 'Will you go and live there?'

'In theory, we'd love to,' said Julia. 'But you can't live in a theory. It's crumbling. No, we'll sell it. Apparently the ornamental lake is one of a very few of its kind, which makes it valuable. There are some developers interested.'

'I want to live there,' said Vita. 'I don't care.'

'Why not,' said Lazarenko, 'if you'd like to?'

'Well, it's falling down,' said Julia. 'Woodworm, dry rot, leaking roof.'

'I see.'

'And then, of course, my daughter set fire to the cellar.'

Lazarenko nodded seriously. 'There's that, yes.' But his eyes were beginning to shine with the light of an idea taking shape.

'I am looking for somewhere to settle, you know,' he said. 'Somewhere for the winters. Arkady needs to be in one place, to work with his creatures. I've been moving him for too long. I'm looking for somewhere to train the young ones, scout for new talent: a school.'

'I didn't know that, no,' said Julia.

'I was thinking, perhaps somewhere upstate,' said Lazarenko. 'Somewhere on the Hudson. Somewhere with space for the children to run.' He smiled at Vita. 'But the place I have in mind would need work. And it would need someone to oversee that work – and to manage things, when I am away. Hypothetically, would you and Mr Welles be interested in such a job?'

'But ... you don't know me,' said Julia.

'Vita has a formidable organisational mind. I assume, from what she says, it must be from you. How would you feel, hypothetically?'

'Hypothetically?' said Julia, and she took in a vast breath of air. 'Hypothetically, I can imagine nothing more hypothetically wonderful.'

'Good,' said Lazarenko. 'I shall write a non-hypothetical cheque.'

There was a general agreement that the IMPERIUM tortoise did not need to be returned to its owner.

And, in the midst of the confusion, Grandpa took Vita's passport to the police station, and explained that the other tortoise it was holding as evidence belonged to his granddaughter. The proof of owner-ship was right there, spelled out in rubies on the tortoise's back.

With the greatest care, Arkady plucked the jewels off the two shells with Vita's tweezers and tipped them into her hands. They weren't, it turned out, nearly as valuable as they looked; like a great deal that had belonged to Sorrotore, they were largely show. But there was enough: enough to buy one small elephant, and to put it on a boat to a sanctuary in India, where nobody would trouble it with iron-pointed rods, and it would be left alone, among the deep green and the high skies it had been born to.

It was spring when they set out from Carnegie Hall. They went on foot to the train station, and for once New York City stopped in its tracks. It turned and stared to watch them go. A waiter froze with his finger in his nose. A pair of young men put down their briefcases and gawped. A toddler no taller than a

Labrador gave a shriek of joy and went running down the street after them.

They went in their flying colours: Arkady in red. Cork walked at his heels, nipping at his hand if he paid too much attention to the two German Shepherds walking on his other side. A crow rode on each shoulder. Moscow came behind, unridden, bedecked in white ribbons, occasionally dipping her muzzle to Arkady's ear.

Silk came in her training clothes: a leotard, wrap cardigan and skirt. She refused to take them off, and they had to be prised from her for laundry days. Her hair was brushed out and freshly washed. It fell, the white-gold of faraway suns, shining, to her waist.

Julia Marlowe walked with Morgan Kawadza. Both gave an arm to Grandpa.

Samuel wore sky-blue trousers, a singlet, and black practice shoes. His wary expression had not gone – it never would, until the day he died (not world-famous as he deserved, but also not alone. The year after his death, his grandson danced at Carnegie Hall). But Samuel had the look, that day, of someone who knows

316

what it is to fly. He did not travel on the pavement – it was a day to remember, and so to fix it in his memory, he spun from the top of one lamp post to another, slid across the roofs of cars: flew.

Vita wore her red silk boots, and her red skirt, and at her throat a necklace of green glass.

They boarded the train at Grand Central Station, taking up an entire carriage. The horse caused a small uproar, but nothing insurmountable.

When the train pulled into the tiny station – unfamiliar in the bright sunlight – the children looked, automatically, to Vita. But she drew back, and Grandpa stalked forwards, halting on his stick.

'This way.' They clambered into cabs and drove out along paved roads, Arkady riding alongside on Moscow, Cork and the German Shepherds trotting behind. They got out at the beginning of a dirt road and walked past briar roses cascading down into the dust, past birds calling and replying overhead.

Vita grinned at Arkady, at Silk and Samuel, and left them, moving to take her grandfather's arm and keep pace with him.

317

'Rapscallion,' he said, and his voice was very low. 'What if it's impossible?'

'What if what is?'

'What if I can't go home, without her?' he said. He looked up at the castle, across the lake. 'She was my home. How can I return without her?'

Vita had no words, for there were none. She only held his arm tighter.

They climbed into boats, and crossed to the jetty, and walked towards the gate into the garden. Grandpa's legs quivered, and he reached out for the gate to steady himself. He raised a foot, put it down again.

Vita was suddenly terrified he would not be able to go in; that his legs or his heart had failed him. She made to step forwards – but he reached into his breast pocket, and from it he drew the picture.

'You and me, girl,' he said.

And Lizzy raised an eyebrow back at him from the photograph.

And he smiled, and stepped into the garden, blooming now in every colour, with red roses springing up the walls.

318

They walked down the path towards the walled garden, Vita leading, her mother after, the circus following. They went in. The fountain was alive now, cascading water up among a sea of roses, and in front of it there was a plaque.

Nobody spoke. Then Vita read it aloud.

'Elizabeth Ailsa Welles. Beloved, beloved, beloved.'

Grandfather stood, his head bowed. A tear dropped down his cheeks and wet the dry ground.

Samuel moved first. Slowly, almost noiselessly, he began to turn backwards and backwards through the flowers, flipping at walking pace, his hands in the soil. Arkady followed him, and then Silk, a trio that had always spoken with their hands and their feet, dancing as if they had just that second invented bravery.

Grandpa leaned on Vita's shoulder, and used her strength to straighten his spine; and her left leg shook but she stood firm under the weight. He looked at the plaque as if memorising its every scratch and line. He turned to watch the children spinning through the grass, and then up at his home, and, last, down at his granddaughter, who stared up at him, her face ferocious with love.

'What a thing you've done, Rapscallion!' he said. He pushed her towards the dancers. 'Go and join them.'

He watched her go, leaping, limping, casting up the earth under her feet. He blinked, long and slow.

His eyes, when he opened them, were those of a man who has wandered in a barren land; of one who has, against all odds, rediscovered something like abundance.

'What a thing!' he said. 'What a miraculous, unthinkable, unsensible thing!' And he thumped his stick on the summer earth, and started towards the house.

ACKNOWLEDGEMENTS

I always think, *this next book will be easier*, and I'm always impressively wrong: that it exists at all is down to the following people. I owe more to them than I can say.

To Ellen Holgate, my editor at Bloomsbury, and Claire Wilson, my agent, I owe my greatest thanks. Both are endlessly sharp-eyed and sharp-minded, and wildly generous; they have been the two greatest strokes of luck in my professional life.

To everyone at Bloomsbury, and in particular Fliss Stevens, for wrestling with the labyrinthine entity that this text became.

To everyone at Simon & Schuster USA, for such discerning editing and for making Vita's walks through New York geographically plausible.

To my big brother, for being such an unfailingly kind reader, and for pointing out my near-clinical addiction to the Oxford comma. To my mother and father, for everything and for always.

To the wonderful community of children's writers in the UK, and especially Cat Doyle, Abi Elphinstone, Kiran Millwood Hargrave, Ross Montgomery, Lauren St John, Piers Torday, Katherine Woodfine and Katie Webber.

To my gang of young readers, who made superb suggestions and were far kinder about the book than I had any right to hope for.

To Cerrie Burnell, who read the manuscript early: I am enormously indebted to her kindness. To Tlotlo Tsamaase and Marcus Ramtohul, who acted as perceptive and generous sensitivity readers.

To Dmitri Levitin, for acting as my Russian authority; Max McGuinness, my New York specialist, and Jeremy Seysses, who ensured that the wine my villain drinks is of the best possible vintage.

To the trapeze teachers at the Gorilla Circus Flying Trapeze School, who taught me to spin upside down by the knees.

And to Charles Collier, who walked with me over a hundred miles of countryside, talking about stolen gems and unruly children, and who told me so much about the story that I did not know.

Have you read

Winner of the Costa Children's Book Award 2017

'Utterly splendid ... Katherine Rundell is now
unarguably in the first rank'
Philip Pullman

Turn the page for an extract ...

FLIGHT

Like a man-made magic wish, the aeroplane began to rise.

The boy sitting in the cockpit gripped his seat and held his breath as the plane climbed into the arms of the sky. Fred's jaw was set with concentration, and his fingers twitched, following the movements of the pilot beside him: joystick, throttle.

The aeroplane vibrated as it flew faster into the setting sun, following the swerve of the Amazon River below them. Fred could see the reflection of the six-seater plane, a spot of black on the vast sweep of blue, as it sped towards Manaus, the city on the water. He brushed his hair out of his eyes and pressed his forehead against the window.

Behind Fred sat a girl and her little brother. They had the same slanted eyebrows and the same brown skin, the same long eyelashes. The girl had been shy, hugging her parents until the last possible moment at the airfield; now she was staring down at the water, singing under her breath, her brother trying to eat his seatbelt.

In the next row, on her own, sat a pale girl with blonde hair down to her waist. Her blouse had a neck-ruffle that came up to her chin, and she kept tugging it down and grimacing. She was determinedly not looking out of the window.

The airfield they had just left had been dusty and almost deserted, just a strip of tarmac under the ferocious Brazilian sun. Fred's cousin had insisted that he wear his school uniform and cricket jumper, and now, inside the hot, airless cabin, he felt like he was being gently cooked inside his own skin.

The engine gave a whine, and the pilot frowned and tapped the joystick. He was old and soldierly, with brisk nostril hair and a grey waxed moustache which seemed to reject the usual laws of gravity. He touched the throttle and the plane soared upwards, higher into the clouds.

It was almost dark when Fred began to worry. The pilot began to belch, first quietly, then violently and repeatedly. His hand jerked, and the plane dipped suddenly to the left. Someone screamed behind Fred. The plane lurched away from the river and over the canopy. The pilot grunted, gasped and wound back the throttle, slowing the engine. He gave a cough that sounded like a choke.

Fred stared at the man – he was turning the same shade of grey as his moustache. 'Are you all right, sir?' he asked. 'Is there something I can do?'

Fighting for breath, the pilot shook his head. He reached over to the control panel and cut the engine. The roar ceased. The nose of the plane dipped downwards. The trees rose up.

'What's happening?' asked the blonde girl sharply. 'What's he doing? Make him stop!'

The little boy in the back began to shriek. The pilot grasped Fred's wrist hard for a single moment, then his head slumped against the dashboard.

And the sky, which had seconds before seemed so reliable, gave way.

THE GREEN DARK

Fred wondered, as he ran, if he was dead. *But*, he thought, *death would surely be quieter*. The roar of the flames and his own blood vibrated through his hands and feet.

The night was black. He tried to heave in breath to shout for help as he ran but his throat was too dry and ashy to yell. He jabbed his finger into the back of his tongue to summon up spit. 'Is anybody there? Help! Fire!' he shouted.

The fire called back in response; a tree behind him sent up a fountain of flames. There was a rumble of thunder. Nothing else replied.

A burning branch cracked, spat red, and fell in a cascade of sparks. Fred leapt away, stumbling backwards into the dark and smacking his head against something hard. The branch landed exactly where he'd been standing seconds before. He swallowed the bile that rose in his throat and began to run again, faster and wilder.

Something landed on his chin, and he ducked, smacking at his face, but it was only a raindrop.

The rain came suddenly and hard. It turned the soot and sweat on his hands to something like tar, but it began to quench the fire. Fred slowed his run to a jog, then to a stop. Gasping, choking, he looked back the way he had come.

The little aeroplane was in the trees. It was smoking, sending up clouds of white and grey into the night sky.

He stared around, dizzy and desperate, but he couldn't see or hear a single human, only the fernlike plants growing around his ankles, and the trees reaching hundreds of feet up into the sky, and the panicked dive and shriek of birds. He shook his head, hard, trying to banish the shipwreck-roar in his ears.

The hair on his arms was singed and smelt of eggs. He put his hand to his forehead; his eyebrow had charred and part of it came away on his fingers. He wiped his eyebrow on the sleeve of his shirt.

Fred looked down at himself. One leg of his trousers was ripped all the way up to the pocket, but none of his bones felt broken. There was vicious pain, though, in his back and neck, and it made his arms and legs feel far-off and foreign.

A voice came suddenly from the dark. 'Who's there? Get away from us!'

Fred spun round. His ears still buzzing, he grabbed a rock from the ground and hurled it in the direction of the voice. He ducked behind a tree and crouched on his haunches, poised to jump or run.

His heart sounded like a one-man band. He tried not to exhale.

The voice said, 'For God's sake, don't throw things!'

It was a girl's voice.

Fred looked out from behind the tree. The light of the moon filtered deep green to the forest floor, casting long-fingered shadows against the trees, and he could see only two bushes, both of them rustling.

'Who is it? Who's there?' The voice came from the second bush.

Fred squinted through the dark, feeling the remaining hair rise up on his arms.

'Please don't hurt us,' said the bush. The accent wasn't British; it was something softer, and the voice was definitely a child's, not an adult's. 'Was it you, throwing poo?'

Fred looked down at the ground. He'd snatched up a piece of years-old, fossilised animal dung.

'Oh,' he said. 'Yes.' He was becoming accustomed to the dark, and could see the shine of eyes peering out from the grey-green gloom of the undergrowth. 'Are you from the plane? Are you hurt?'

'*Yes*, we're hurt! We fell out of the sky!' said one bush, as the other said, 'No, not badly.'

11

'You can come out,' said Fred. 'It's only me here.'

The second bush parted. Fred's heart gave a great leap. Both the girl and her brother were covered in scratches and burns and ash – which had mixed with sweat and rain and made a kind of paste on their faces – but they were alive. He was not alone. 'You survived!' he said.

'Obviously we did,' said the first bush, 'or we'd be less talkative, wouldn't we?' The blonde girl stepped out into the lashing rain. She stared from Fred to the other two, unsmiling. 'I'm Con,' she said. 'It's short for Constantia, but if you call me that I'll kill you.'

Fred glanced at the other girl. She smiled nervously, and shrugged. 'Right,' he said. 'If you say so. I'm Fred.'

'I'm Lila,' said the second girl. She held her brother on her hip. 'And this is Max.'

'Hi.' Fred tried to smile but it made the cuts on his cheek stretch and burn so he stopped and made do with a grin that involved only the left half of his face.

Max was at the breathless stage of crying, and he clung to his sister so tightly his fingers were pressing

12

bruises on her skin. She was leaning over to one side to hold him up, shaking with the effort. They looked, Fred thought, like a two-headed creature, arms entwined.

'Is your brother badly hurt?' he asked.

Lila patted her brother desperately on the back. 'He won't talk – he's just crying.'

Con looked back towards the fire and shivered. The flames cast a light on her face. She was no longer blonde; her hair was grey with soot and brown with blood, and she had a scratch on her shoulder that looked deep.

'Are you all right?' he asked, wiping rain out of his eyes. 'That cut looks bad.'

'No, I'm not all right,' Con spat. 'We're lost, in the Amazon jungle, and statistically speaking it's very likely that we're going to die.'

Books to feed the imagination.
Go on an adventure with

KATHERINE RUNDELL

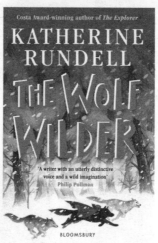

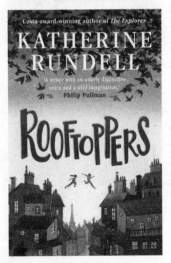

For younger readers

A gloriously illustrated story
that brings the magic of Christmas to life

For grown-up readers

KATHERINE
RUNDELL

Why You Should
Read Children's
Books,

Even Though You Are
So Old and Wise

BLOOMSBURY

An unmissable essay about
the importance of children's literature

ABOUT THE AUTHOR

Katherine Rundell is the bestselling author of five children's novels and has won the Costa Children's Book Award, the Blue Peter Book Award and the Waterstones Children's Book Prize amongst many others. Her novels are now published in thirty countries. Katherine spent her childhood in Africa and Europe before taking her degree at the University of Oxford and becoming a Fellow of All Souls College. As well as writing, she studies Renaissance literature and is learning, very slowly, to fly a small aeroplane.